A Morsel of Hope
The Refuge

To Dani, thank you for your invaluable advice, feedback and support.

To Jim, thank you for your helpful comments, patience and encouragement.

Blinding bright light...rumbling sound...the ground shakes, then a train just passes by...the problem is there isn't any railroad close by. This keeps the patrons away from my parents' diner. If this stays on, then soon they will lose the business. I'm Tally McDowell, 37 years old, and am desperate for clues...

CHAPTER 1

The Presence

Present Day 2029

Finally, the first breeze of fall has arrived! And this is also the time when the atmosphere outside turns dull as if mourning the arrival of autumn when most flowers and trees will lose their leaves and some may even die. Suddenly I am hit with homesickness. I grew up in Minnesota in a small quiet town of Oakland. It is pretty much where you get to enjoy a slow-paced country lifestyle but at the same time full of life that is illuminated by the ever beautiful vibrant autumn colors of the leaves. The best contrast in life that I enjoyed when I was growing up. Even a park full of screaming kids I find soothing to hear, for it represents safe ground and respect for life.

My current address now is in the Twin Cities where the hustle and bustle of big city life still overwhelms me. My unit is on the 5th floor of a ten-story condominium building on the eastside of the industrial center of the city. This is not that far from my parents' new home in Silverlake Village east of Oakland. I still get to enjoy a relaxing suburban break from fast-paced city life whenever I visit them in their tame world. I guess the reason why I never go far away from suburbs is that I still anticipate meeting the right guy and seeing myself having a perfect suburban family life here in Minnesota. I'm a hopeless dreamer, I guess. Anyway, this is also the time of the year that I get busy planning for my winter vacation with my two best friends. Someplace warm and sandy. So, as I'm looking through the jumble on my desk for the latest travel magazine I received in the mail, the phone rings. It's my mother and it's 9:00 pm.

~ 0 ~

One Year Ago

My parents sold our old house in Oakland Town which they found a bit oversized for just the two of them since I moved out 15 years ago. And together with their retirement money, my parents bought the first land put on-sale on the block of Circle Drive in old downtown of Silverlake, a small, nice, charming town north of where I live. Everyone knew everybody by face if not by name. They wanted to stay in the community of their roots, the place where they grew up and this was where they planned to retire. So, when they bought this land it was heaven on earth for them. And the only way to keep living their dream was to build a source of income and at the same time something to keep them busy. Soon they had the ribbon-cutting of a new diner they named "The Cottage Cafe" and a blessing of their new cottage-style house adjacent to the diner.

It wasn't that hard for the café to be

7

accepted, and as the old downtown wanted to keep and support only local businesses, they already got the approval. This was the most comfortable eatery you could ever imagine, with homey dining area, furnished with white-finish wooden furniture, antique-style silverware, white ruffled curtains and adobe stoned walls and floor. The diner was around 300 square feet with eight tables, a small bar and a kitchen at the back. It was just right for the two of them to handle with a few helpers.

My mother, Anita, now 67, included her home-style cooking in the menu. My father, John, who just turned 69, managed the café. He loved the work for he got to continue practicing his last job as a hotel manager in one of the local hotels in the suburb. And as the only child, a consultant in a marketing and advertising company, all I could contribute was my unending support and love. It was a promising small business and expected to sustain itself if not compete against big restaurants. Surely every week, there were families that would stay away from the mess of cooking at their own kitchens. That was the case for six months until one night when a bizarre incident slowed the business down. On that night, the patrons were enjoying their meal when the room was illuminated with a bright light, appeared to be coming through the window from straight across the distance. And this was followed by progressively louder sounds! Everybody at the diner thought that it was a tornado and ran for safety behind the counter. The ground seemed to shake and in an instance a train passed through the window above their heads and out through the back wall. Everybody froze and blood drained out of their faces.

My father broke the tension by saying, "Um, hot coffee and pie on the house!!!"

Still dazed, nobody paid attention to what he offered and everybody bolted out except for one grandpa who was smart enough to grab a pie before running to the door. Of course, my parents didn't have a choice but to stay put and let the shock clear out of their systems.

~ *0* ~

Thursday, September 13; it's rare that I get calls from my parents at around 9 pm since this is the time they clean up and close the diner. A bit concerned, I pick up the phone, and right away my mother starts talking on the other line like she's being chased by a tiger. I ask her to slow down because I don't get what she just said.

"We just had a train at the diner!" she says in a high-pitched tone.

"You mean a kid brought a toy train or someone just came over to sell you a decorative train?" I ask, trying to give her multiple choices to make it less complicated.

"No! A ghost!" she loudly utters, sounding impatient. "A spirit of a runaway train right inside the diner."

When it becomes clear what she says just happened at the diner, I laugh. But she is not laughing at the other line and I could even feel the choking in her voice and shaking in her body and that's when it hits me that she is serious.

"Okay," I calmly say. "I'll take a day off tomorrow and come over to check on it." That seems to calm down my mother and she hangs up.

This I have to see for myself. A real car that accidentally hits and wrecks the café is more within my mental grasp than what my mother just described. So, I take a day off the next day and hang at the diner and help them get some work done at the same time.

None of the customers who witnessed the incident have attempted to tell anyone about it, fearing that people would think that they're crazy. Anyway, no one can make any sense of what happened either.

Tonight, we only have one couple in their 70's and I seated them in the corner table away from the main window at the front of the diner. The woman has her back to the wall facing me. I'm sitting at the table directly across the window in the center of the eating area.

So, as darkness falls, I notice while staring out the window a light that starts to get bigger and brighter followed by loud thundering sounds and rumbling in the floors.

"There's an earthquake!" shouts the woman in the corner.

The man with her immediately goes under the table. The woman quickly follows.

I stand a little shaken, but feet firm on the ground. I know this will not physically hit the diner so I have to keep my eyes on the window and not dare to blink so as not to miss whatever it is. There, right in front of me is a train coming straight at me. It seems so real that I duck to avoid it when it passes above my head and is gone like smoke when it hits the wall behind me. I didn't even notice if there was anybody on it. I don't think this train is driving through just to order an omelet.

I look back at my father standing behind the counter. He seems relaxed now, he just raises his eyebrows at me, then sips his coffee. Then my mother comes running out from the kitchen wiping her hands on her apron like she just finished cleaning up and asks me, "So, did you see it? What do you think it was?"

Without waiting for me to answer, she spots the couple under the corner table and runs to them and helps them come out of their hiding.

This doesn't happen every night, but who would want to take the risk of getting spooked while drinking hot coffee? Who would enjoy such a live ghost show with a meal? Nobody!

The next thing we know, the Cottage Café is given the name The Haunted Café by the locals who had witnessed the presence, and that would be most of the town's small population. People can't resist glancing at the diner whenever they happen to pass by whether by car or by foot. My parents sometimes see people taking pictures of the diner. No big deal if they're treating it as a tourist attraction to recommend to friends, but it turns out that those are the believers of such phenomenon. They take pictures in hopes of capturing an image of the train. In some cases, out of desperation, they take even the tiniest imperfection of printing the pictures as proofs of its existence.

Weeks pass, and the Cottage is slowly losing its patrons. My parents are slowly losing hope that they can keep the diner any longer. It's really hard to fight a battle when you can't touch your adversary. The most logical reaction to this is to scream and run away. But you can't just pack the diner up like a picnic basket and run, so we are stuck with it. My parents are at their wits' end. Their dreams and lives are in this place. I'm not going to just watch this train wreck our lives right in front of me, when I know that I can do something, or at the least investigate what is causing it. The stakes are too high to just sit back and enjoy the show. If losing this café will break my parents' hearts, then derailing this train is the only way to go. I guess I have to kiss my vacation goodbye for this year.

CHAPTER 2

Follow the Tracks

Who would think to ask if by chance there's any ghost living at the property you're dreaming to own? No one that I know of! But the deal is done and my parents are stuck with the property with no return and refund policy under such condition. So, when there's a ghost there's a past life, right? The easiest and traditional way to resolve this kind of problem is to talk to the ghost and ask what it wants to accomplish here on earth to be able to move on. But, did I mention that my ghost is a train which can't think and talk back? So, I guess I have to do this the hard way.

It's Saturday, October 6; nothing like researching anything under the sun from the comfort of my own couch. I have all weekend to learn a bit about the town's train history or any train incidents, thanks to the internet. So to start with, I search *train incidents in Silverlake, Minnesota;* and it gives me zero match searched. Next, I tweak, scramble, switch and add more possible terms connected to my town's train mishaps in the past, still zero result. *Hmm*, I didn't expect it to be that tricky. It turns out that I only consumed thirty minutes of my whole weekend with that search. I have to stick to my plan of getting some answers to this unorthodox sighting happening right in my parents' yard today and tomorrow for some peace of mind.

Visiting the local library is not a bad idea. I get to see the people in my community and maybe chat with one or two to keep me up to date with what's going on around me. And at the same time show my support that justifies the physical existence of such iconic structure in our society. With everything wirelessly accessible and most people, even kids as young as two years old, have walking bookshelves right in their tablets nowadays, it devalues the importance of public libraries that were valuable resources in the past and now primitive in the present. I finish my coffee, change my clothes then stuff my bag with pen and paper for whatever notes I'll need to jot down.

It's a good timing. When I get there, the library just opens. Then I can get all the help I need without any wait time or long lines or suspicious grumpy tired tones asking me, *why am I being so nosey that they have to dig in the back of the archive section just for train records.*

After browsing all the books, journals and maps of Silverlake's historical records, I finally get a train. But it was only mentioned in passing, and it's the one in Oakland town which I've known all my life. To be exact, it's about 8 miles NW of the diner. That's as close as I can get to a train! Now what? Why is the ghost train taking a detour to my parent's property? I'm not prepared for what I think is the more complex research that this entails to unlock the mystery behind it.

Too engrossed with my digging, I didn't notice that someone snuck a note in my bag. It reads, 'What consumes you is now 6 ft. below the ground! END'.

Looking around, I don't find anybody suspicious or anything out of place or maybe I just don't know what I need to look for. Well, if this note implies a grave then that's a given since I'm dealing with a ghost right now but what puzzles me is how did someone know that I am looking into something like this? I guess this is my cue to call it a day.

That night, I think about that note and who dropped it in my bag. Like my grandmother always said when I was a kid, "Don't be afraid of a ghost because it can't hurt you; be more afraid of a person with bad intention."

Now which one should I deal with first; the train that just spooks people or my unknown sender, who is a total mystery of what he or she wants from me. Next thing you know I dose off to sleep not making a choice.

When I wake up the next day, my mind clears up and I realize that this is the time when my parents need me the most. For now, this takes higher priority. So yes, even a stalker can't stop me from cleaning up this unwanted visitor off my parents' yard. I guess my mystery stranger will have to wait to get the satisfaction of gaining the attention from me.

Here I am again, the first Sunday in November, my supposed weekend to relax; I'm off to the Library of Minnesota in Roseville to check their archives. It takes me two and a half hours to drive there. I thought I graduated from going to libraries the moment I graduated from college; well, never say never as they always say.

After the incident at the old town's library, I feel that I'm not alone anymore. I have to glance at my rear mirror more often than usual and mentally record every car that is behind me. I get to the library's parking lot in time to find a car pulling out of a space so close to the entrance and I grab that space to stay in a safe zone where no one would attempt to do something crazy to me with a big chance of getting mobbed. At the library, I find the archive of newspapers of important events that happened in Silverlake dating way back 1992. Great! Finally, I'm going to tackle first the significant events that made the history, then down to the small incidents. But before I start, something stops me. The year 1992 doesn't make sense. All neighboring towns started with year as early as 1950 and only the Silverlake village archive starts with the year 1992. What about before that? Were we ignored? Is it possible that nothing major happened in the prior years or the entire pile of newspapers is someplace else? There must be at least one major event that is worthy to go down in the history of our town in the prior years. So, I walk up to a librarian and ask her if they have the missing years somewhere?

She looks it up on the computer and says, "Our records show no entries prior 1992. That's all there is."

Then I ask, "How is it possible that the neighboring towns around us have records back 1950 and not Silverlake?"

She smiles and nicely says, "If I were you I would go to the national library. Then maybe they'll have more records at hand since they have much more space."

"But do libraries still keep paper records instead of having them digitally archived?" I ask politely, hoping not to bug her.

The woman slowly takes her glasses off and put them down on the counter, looks me straight in the eye and says, "What are the chances of a library catching fire and all documents burning to ash? Heard of any? None, right? But what are the statistics of computers getting corrupted if not wiped cleaned of all contents? A lot! Some critical documents are too important to put at risks of getting deleted. I hope that answers your inquiry."

Beyond that she can't help me anymore. I walk back to my table with one question stuck in my mind, "Why just Silverlake?" And there it is again, waiting on my seat is a note. I ask a few people seating in the next table if they saw anyone dropping the note or getting close to my chair? And as expected, no one saw anything because stalkers seem to have a school that hones their skill of invisibility.

This time the note doesn't make any sense 'N42.665706 W83.158137. END'. There's my cue again. But before I head to my car, I have to wait for somebody to walk along with to the parking lot just to be safe. Luckily, I see a middle-aged man putting his backpack on and grabbing his books. I stand by the exit and quietly walk close behind him to the parking lot. Upon spotting my car, I run and hop in then press the lock-all-doors button. Before reaching home, I need to do one more thing, a drive through at a fast-food restaurant for a meal. I hardly ever do this, since I can easily prepare food for myself at home, but I have to test if any car will follow me on the route I'm going to take. I got my order and just one minivan with a kid seated in the middle row is behind me. I'm out and so far my rear mirror is clear.

When I get in to my apartment building, I straight away access the stairs and dash to my unit in a record-breaking time. I immediately lock the door behind me, secure the chain door lock, and turn off all lights except the one outside my unit, and not even a window open to let the fresh air in. I have to sleep on the couch where I always feel nestled and comforted in my times of stress and worries after a hard day. The view of the dark sky with all the shining stars and the moonlight gives me a sense of calm and peace. That night while lying down, I thought of moving in with my parents until I figure out what the ghost train wanted but then I shoot it down for the reason that I don't want them to get in the middle of my situation right now. I have not told them about my stalker, not to add to their worries. Suddenly, the letters and numbers on the note pop up in my head and I could even visualize them floating in the air. Finally, those memory pills are paying off. The codes are latitude and longitude! But of what? I get up, run to my computer and enter the coordinates on an online site that gives a specific location anywhere on Earth based on coordinates. Voila! It's where my parents' diner and house are situated.

Still, I can't see what my stalker is trying to tell me. I can't wait for tomorrow to come. I will be presenting my team's concept to market a steel company in order to secure good will and more investment. Also, that will be a good break for me from all of these weird events.

In the middle of my presentation, it suddenly hits me while looking at my male bosses, *what if one of these guys is my stalker?* I don't realize that I'm staring blankly at them as if forgotten what to say for a few seconds until one of my teammates coughs to get my attention.

The big bosses are supposed to ask questions

and give comments after each team presentation to sift the details and help refine the finished product before the submission to the client. Well…we don't get any. It only means two things, one is there were no holes to patch which I doubt after giving them unpleasant stare; or two, I fumbled so bad that there's no point to waste their time with questioning. The ghost train and my stalker are taking a toll on my career now.

My weekdays pass and this seems to be the longest week of my life. I have to be wary of everything around me. Every step I make I have to be on guard and glance over my shoulder to make sure no one's tailing me. I never experienced such extreme paranoia in my life and it feels like an electric shock that changes the course of everything in me and literally changing the rate of my heartbeat with my every move. This feeling keeps me up most of the nights and gives me the determination to solve the ghost problem without delay then tackle my stalker.

I didn't have any luck with the local and state libraries, maybe I'll be able to dig something up at the Federal Library. It's like a bolt of highly regarded documents and they keep materials of utmost important to the nation, down to the state level. So, who said I won't be traveling this year?

Now I'm excited that I can mix business with pleasure! On Friday, November 9; I book my flight to Washington, DC and I get there the next day. I rent a car with the built-in Wi-Fi hotspots. In cars nowadays, travel has never been more convenient. Since I'm always connected, directions and emails don't add to my worries. They even have the call forwarding feature. I just punch in my phone number and calls come in anytime.

I arrive in time at my hotel to check-in. Then not to waste any minute, I work my way to the library and begin my inquest. This time, I don't bother to bring my bag with me so as to avoid unwanted drop-offs. I only take with me a notebook and a pen; my wallet in one pocket of my coat and keys in the other.

I start my way to the maps. I find the Oakland town, to its north is Sandstone, and to the south of it is Pine City. To the east of Oakland is already the lake. But where is Silverlake on the map? This document was printed in 1920 and it only means that this is the original structure of these towns in eastern Minnesota.

I look back over the map to assure what I'm seeing is true. Silverlake is not on the map! I don't care if this is official but I don't think this map is right. It could have been misprinted. The one in the local library has more details than this. Well, it's not going to hurt to have a copy of this map and compare it with my local map. Now moving to the archive section, as the librarian told me that I have to search the articles on their website then write down the reference number of the specific material before she can pull it out of the archive room. When I type in Silverlake, Minnesota 1950, 1990 on the search field, it gives zero result. Then, I just enter the keywords, "Minnesota, train, mishap". Then appears a fair number of articles alphabetically arranged by city! I don't see any Silverlake listing but there was indeed one incident that happened in the neighboring town of Oakland in 1990. The article mentioned a train accident caused by a mild earthquake with all five passengers including the operator suffering only minor injuries.

Suddenly I feel a pat on my back. A girl in her pre-teens with beautiful, wavy, dark brown hair and stylish glasses is handing me a folded paper and says, "A man told me that you dropped this paper."

"Huh! Which man?" I quickly look around to check who she's referring to, but don't see one. When I turn back to face her, she's already leaving in a hurry not to be left behind by her class group. "Wait!"

I try to chase her but the adult in charge of the group looks at me like I'm a deranged woman about to steal an egg from the nest. So I stop the pursuit.

I open the paper and the note reads, "You have to dig deeper to find out the truth. END". Oh come on! I have had enough of this! This only happens to a character in a movie. How can he know where I am? One tiny clue is revealed though, that my stalker is a man. But I can't ignore the fact that all the messages made some sense. Could this mean that they are connected? Could this stalker be also a ghost that was on the train? Well, if he follows me here and watches my every move, then I can't do anything about it for now. I will not run away and drop my research, not this far and with the money I spent already coming here.

I continue on to look up for just *Minnesota, Silverlake* without any year or additional word to widen the search. And there…records of events in Silverlake finally got noted. But then again, I notice the date of the first incident was in 1992. And to add to my disappointment, nothing about train accident or even an existence of any train is listed! I get so sucked into my browsing that I forgot about the time.

It's a quarter past four in the afternoon. I need to pick up Kate. I gather all the materials I have out and ask the staff at the service desk to hold them for me since I'm from out of town and will be coming back the next day. Thank goodness she is so accommodating and agrees to it.

This trip is not all business. A little tour won't hurt, I hope. Kate, my best friend, is flying from Minnesota to meet me here in DC for a short weekend vacation. We both have not been here, and since I cancelled our out-of-the-country trip for this year she is settling for this rather than nothing at all. She also knows that I'm helping my parents sort out this mysterious ghost train. But, I have not shared the part that I attracted a shadow that follows me and sends me notes every now and then. She's a little over dramatic and might get paranoid about every innocent person following behind us. My stalker has not done anything that I should be alarmed about, aside from few intriguing notes. The worst thing I can get from them is paper cut, which is actually irritating to get, though. In short, a little thing can freak out Kate. Also, I named my stalker "Shadow".

Under the laughter, during the entire night of fun bar-hopping with Kate, is a lost feeling of *what am*

I going to do next? It feels that I hit a dead end with my research. But, I don't let my frustration ruin the vacation for me and my friend.

The next day, Sunday, while touring around the city, I spot one attraction that says "SPY". It is a museum of spy gadgets of all sorts. Since it's still a bit early to watch a matinee theatrical play, Kate and I check the place out. During the tour, one thing catches my attention, a GPS. Of course! Why didn't I think of that? While walking around the museum, nothing else is registering to me but questions playing in my mind. Is it possible that my stalker has put a GPS on me? But how and when? And most importantly, where is it right now? What is that constant thing that I can't leave home without? My set of keys? But, my keys are pretty bare and nothing complicated with them. My bag? I change bags every now and then. My car? I'm in rental car right now. Of course, the wallet! I quietly take my wallet out of my pocket to check. This time my friend notices the odd behavior of grabbing my wallet in the middle of the hallway, not of a shopping mall but of a museum. We both never buy any souvenirs from any museums for we know that everything is overpriced. I then tell her that I'm not sure if I put my credit card back after paying at the entrance.

"But we paid in cash, remember?" recalls Kate.

"Oh! Of course," I reply while still looking through my wallet.

It is a scenario that I never imagined to happen to me in this lifetime. To my surprise, there it is! A thin metal object a size of a round tiny watch battery that's hard to find in stores whenever I need one. It is in the inside corner of the coin compartment nestling comfortably. I put it back and will think of what to do next with it.

After watching the play, I have a few hours left to get to the library before it closes.

"Kate, I need to stop by the library to retrieve some materials," I say, trying to ignore the look of disappointment in her face.

"Seriously?! With a few hours left to enjoy the place?" she asks in a disgruntled way.

"Do you want to come?" I ask, still denying her frustration.

"Arrrgh!" she sounds jokingly annoyed. "I might as well do my shopping then I'll meet you back at the hotel."

So, we split up.

At the library, I copy all the articles including the Oakland train accident in 1990 and the original map.

That night we take the red-eye flight back home. Even just the sight of my street gives me a great feeling of being home already. I can't wait! It's a line that never gets old, *home sweet home*. The moment I get inside my apartment, I drop everything and just hit the sack and pass out.

The next morning, I take a day off to get some rest and sort everything out and plan my next move or where to look next. But first, I want some relaxing music, and savor a good breakfast and a cup of freshly brewed coffee. Um, did I just say a cup? I think what I meant to say was a few cups to wake me up.

I receive a free copy of local newspaper in the mail which I don't usually get. Why not? I might come across news about an escape convict hiding in the building. Then that will give me a more valid reason to tell my boss why I'm home. While browsing the newspaper a couple of pages drop off. It's not uncommon to find customized Post-its with ads stuck on one of your mails or journals. What's different with these ones on the loose pages are the written arrows pointing to an article on each page with a note that says, "Please read. END." I closely check the papers and I can't believe what I'm looking at. They are copies of old Oakland Town newspapers dated June 1990 and January 1992. And the highlighted articles on the papers have a picture of a train wreck on one, and a news about what was taken from Oakland Town on the other. Before I get too excited, I have to know what the news is all about. This is more detailed than what I gathered from the national library. Well, Shadow seems to be ahead of me. Now he gets my attention.

The best way to approach all the clues that I have is to compare them. I have one empty wall that I can use to post everything by dividing them into two categories, left half of the wall for local, and the other half for national. And the moment I lay them side by side and incorporate Shadow's notes, it made clear where Silverlake then and now!

CHAPTER 3

Off Track

Summer 1990

Oakland Town, Minnesota, June 4. After Eric Dutton had spent long hours at work on a Monday, 9 pm was about the time to surrender to tiredness and head home before the last passenger train left. He decided to leave his paper work on his desk in disarray thinking he would be back early tomorrow morning anyway. He grabbed his jacket, wallet and keys and headed out. His building was just a block away from the train station and this was one of the reasons why he enjoyed his job downtown as the lead architect in a construction company. His car just sat at the terminal lot and the five minute drive to his home was always a no-sweat routine. There were just five passengers including Eric on the train that night.

The moment he got seated, his eyes started to close and his head fell back on the glass window behind him. Staying up late last night watching the news coverage of the devastation caused by the Lower Ohio Valley Tornado Outbreak that happened two days ago, and the long day at work, made his mind and body eventually surrender to sleep.

He was awakened by light shaking and a gentle bump on the back of his head that was caused by the curve on the tracks. Being a light sleeper, any slight disturbance could wake him up. When he opened his eyes, he realized that he just missed his stop. The next stop was the second to last terminal. And he guessed all the other four passengers were getting off at the last terminal since nobody was preparing to get off. He stood up at the exit door and held onto the steel post. While staring into the darkness outside, the train started to get a little bumpy. He didn't know if it was a normal run at this portion of the track since he had never been past his terminal before. His grip on the post got firmer. Then he heard a loud screech, followed by a sudden hard thud and he knew and felt that the train was off the track.

The passengers were jolted. The train started to tilt 45 degrees while skidding off track. Everyone was tossed and knocked out except Eric who had a strong grip at the metal handle. He closed his eyes but stayed alert and waiting for everything to stop. Finally, the train stopped, but it did with a hard tug, as if something suddenly held it down from behind.

It was pitch black around him and he could tell that their train was resting on its side. The side of his head hurt and his right foot was stuck between the loose seat and a metal frame that held it, but other than that he didn't feel any broken bones or cuts. He slowly pushed the seat with his left foot while at the same time holding on the metal frame firm to widen the gap between them. With some tugging of his right foot, he was able to free it. It felt a little bruised from getting squeezed but he could still move it fine. He stood up and that's when he knew he wasn't injured.

Now he had the hard task of checking on the other four passengers in the dark and in the wreckage. He needed to know how they were doing.

"Hello! Can anybody hear me?" he shouted.

He heard a moan not far from him.

"Over here!" a struggling voice called out.

He went down on all fours and cautiously crawled to where the sound was coming from. As he was feeling the things in front of him as he moved, he finally touched a foot. Then, he realized that it belonged to an unconscious passenger piled on top of the one moaning.

"Are you ok?" he asked to the passenger underneath.

With a struggle in his voice he answered, "I can't move and I feel numb on my body. I'm struggling to breathe because of a hard pressure on my chest."

Eric told him that there was another person on top of him that he didn't want to move. He also told the man that he could make the injuries worse.

"Hang on. I'll get help right away," assured Eric.

Before he left, the man said, "My name is David Smith and I need you to please call my wife Anne and let her know what happened and not to worry."

He thought to himself that *who wouldn't freak out when 'train' and 'accident' were use in one sentence?*

After the man gave his home phone number, he committed to him that it would be done. He thought that it was the least thing he could do to help the man at that moment of uncertainty. Then, he tried to call out to the other passengers but he didn't get any reply. So, he thought it would be best to get help as soon as possible so as not to delay the necessary treatments for everyone. He made his way out through the broken window right on top of him. With the light of the moon, he could see better outside of the train. When he saw that the first car of the train was just one car away; he made a quick effort to check on the engineer. But he wasn't answering, and Eric couldn't see him in the smoke.

Suddenly, Eric felt sick to his stomach. He fell down on his knees and a gush of heat went up in his head. His body started to feel whimsy weird. And then it quickly went away.

He was certain that there was no imminent danger since he didn't smell gas or see fire. He then looked around and saw that there was a lighted roadway north of where they were. He walked around to the other side and passed the nose of the train towards the main road. He saw a clearing on the side of the tracks going west so he took it.

After about 30 yards, he saw a woman seated in the grass with her arms around a boy. The woman looked to be in her forties and the boy around eight years old.

"Are you ok?" he asked softly not to add panic to the situation.

She nodded and said, "We are fine. Watch your step. There's a hole behind you."

Eric thought the boy was hurt because of the elongated dark spot on his left forearm but he wasn't showing any sign that he was in pain. But the boy definitely looked a bit shaken.

"Wait there. I'll call for help," he said.

"No! We're fine and we can make it out of here," the woman was adamant not to get help.

"I saw lights in that direction maybe we can all walk there and get help for the injured," he calmly suggested.

The woman agreed and they walked painstakingly as fast as they could to get to the nearest gas station to call for help. But halfway in their walk, he looked back and saw dozens of emergency vehicles with flashing lights already at the site. *That was fast* he thought to himself. Though it gave him a sigh of relief, he still needed to make an emergency call to make sure.

"By the way, my name is Eric," introducing himself. He was waiting for a counter introduction but they seemed to be aloft and trying to distance themselves.

They got to the gas station in time to see the crew turn off the lights and lock up!

He ran towards a middle-aged man to catch him before he left, leaving the mother and son lagging behind. The man, upon seeing Eric rushing towards him, screamed while surrendering the keys to him, "Please take whatever you want! Don't hurt me. No one will take care of my Mamu."

"I'm not going to hurt you. I just want to use the phone to make an emergency call. We had an accident," Eric explained while holding his hands up in front of the man to show that he wasn't armed.

The man nervously unlocked the door to the store and let him in.

He placed a 911 call and the operator confirmed that help was there already and he didn't need to worry because everything would be taken care of. Then his next call was to David's wife. Unfortunately, nobody was answering the phone.

He didn't think he needed to head to the hospital since he was doing fine and also to avoid any unending questions from reporters if not from medical staff. He never dreamed of sharing his personal data through news broadcast or local papers. He guessed his two companions right now shared the same state of mind.

His next call was to a cab for a ride to pick up his car at the terminal parking lot.

Then, he turned to his two companions and offered them the phone in case they needed to call anybody to pick them up but the woman said they were fine, again. He then said goodbye to them. He faced the store crew and said, "Thank you for the phone calls. I'll come back tomorrow to pay the cost."

The man then said, "Don't worry about it."

"By the way, who's Mamu?" he curiously asked.

"He's my two year old cairn terrier," the man replied.

Eric just smiled at him then stepped outside and waited for his cab.

While waiting, he noticed that the woman and the boy were waiting too, but for what?

The boy discreetly gestured to his mother that it was okay to approach Eric.

After a while, the woman and the boy walked up to him and the woman spoke, "My name is Thea and my son's name is Zian. We just arrived here.

Today was the first day of our move from the south. We don't know anybody around here. We were wondering if you have any small unused space to lend to us for the night. We'll pay you!"

A lot of what-ifs with strangers played in Eric's mind, so he replied, "My place is a bit cramped and I don't…" but before he could finish what he was saying, his cab arrived, "Sorry, I have to go."

When he got in the cab, one thing made clear in his head, the woman needed to make sure that her boy would be safe for the night especially in this unfamiliar place, so for that reason he couldn't just leave them there.

"Come on!" he called out to them.

During the ride, he asked, "Where's the rest of your stuff?"

The woman answered, "We left them behind."

"You mean, back at the crash site?" he asked, trying to better understand what she just said.

"No. Back home because we were in a hurry to leave that we didn't have time to pack, we just took the clothes we have on us and one backpack with some necessities," she replied.

The driver of the cab started to look suspicious, and Eric saw him glaring at Thea through the rear mirror. Well, he couldn't blame him. He, too, didn't like the context of what she just said. He knew there was something arguably scary with the scenario that she just mentioned so for the boy's sake he had to wait until they got off the cab to interrogate further. Thea definitely needed to assure him that they were not trouble before stepping into his place.

Zian looked shy and wasn't making any eye contact with Eric. He wasn't sure if the boy knew what was happening around him or why they needed to ran away from home.

They got off at the front of the terminal parking lot and before they walked toward his car he had to get some details out of her so he asked, "I'm sorry, but I need to know what you are running from? I think I have the right to ask before letting you sleep just a few feet away from me. The boy I trust but it's the running away from something that I don't."

"The place where I came from is not safe for children anymore," she began, "we were living in fear of abuse and intimidation by our leader. He and his supporters seem to have some kind of markings that allow them to get away with whatever mischiefs they do. My husband stayed behind with my older son to join a crusade to put a stop to it all. And when that happens then we can go back home."

That left him speechless and more like sorry for the situation they were in.

When they got home, he grabbed the phone and dialed David's home phone number again. Finally, a woman answered. He introduced himself and told her of what happened and assured her that David was fine. She sounded relieved since she had been waiting up and getting really worried. But she suddenly cried out in pain.

"Is everything ok?" he asked.

What she uttered next was beyond his comprehension.

"I'm pregnant and my baby is coming! Please help me!" she cried.

Because of the accident, Eric still had some adrenalin running in him that he just found himself driving to David's house. He couldn't even remember asking for the home address or leaving his house. A pregnant woman about to give birth was terrifying for him and left him catatonic at some point in the conversation. But at least he remembered telling his guests not to wait up.

The address and bits of directions that he wrote on his palm, pointed him to a three story apartment building. He entered through the main door and looked in the directory to find the location of the apartment number Anne gave him. It was on the second floor so he made his way up.

When he got in front of the apartment unit, it was so quiet that he thought he was at the wrong address. He knocked but nobody answered. Eric thought that maybe somebody got to her first and rushed her to the hospital. He was about to leave when he heard a faint cry. He stopped and listened. Then, more cries. He turned the knob and the door opened. There was Anne, giving him a weak smile and in her arms was her baby. The meeting was not a traditional handshake. For Eric it was overwhelming to describe and yet a special moment to see and experience.

She told him that after she hung up the phone, everything happened so fast.

Anne was a petite woman, five feet two inches tall and weighed 110 pounds. He easily carried her while she held her baby tight. He drove them to the nearest hospital where he assumed that the five injured people from the train accident were taken...but he was wrong.

When Anne and the baby were taken away by the emergency staff, he started to ask around specifically about David Smith. But there wasn't any patient by that name. Nobody had heard of any such accident or even required any urgent assistance in the emergency room for that matter. Eric then thought it was possible that they were taken somewhere else and he just left it at that.

He went back to check on Anne and the doctor and staff assured him that she and the baby were doing fine. He then went to see her in her room to say goodbye. Anne thanked him for all the help that he had extended to them. Before he left, he wrote on the notepad on the side table his phone number in case she needed anything while David was not around.

He got home around three in the morning the next day already. He dropped on the couch and thought to himself that it was the longest day of his life and fell asleep.

CHAPTER 4

What's With the Secrecy?

The next morning, Eric turned the television on to see if any news about the accident was being reported. Most local channels did but it was only mentioned casually like nothing to fuss about. It was concluded that a minor earthquake at the site caused the commuter train to derail and there were no major injuries to any passengers reported. He then checked the local newspaper to see if anything was mentioned about where the passengers were taken for treatment but it was only mentioned as a minor incident and nothing was reported about the passengers.

That day, he left work early and out of curiosity, he drove to the area where the accident happened. There was a mile long blockage on the road from the site. He was stopped by a uniformed man. The man walked towards the front passenger side of his car and he rolled down its window.

The man then said, "You have to turn around and take the detour through the west side of the town."

"But I need to visit a friend at the gas station just a mile ahead," persisted Eric.

"I'm sorry but the only gas station beyond this point is temporarily closed," the uniformed man said firmly. He stepped back not giving him another chance to say a word, then waved his right hand instructing him to back away while the left hand was ready to draw if he dared to roll forward.

Eric turned around and parked half a mile away from the blockage then walked on foot through the woods. He was stopped again but this time by a barbed-wire fence. He crawled under the lowest wire and got scratched on the back. He felt pain like the tip of a knife just ran on the right side of his back. But that was not enough to stop him. He continued on, and after a couple of kilometers he saw a clearing and stayed just behind the big tree to hide himself. Now, he couldn't quite grasp what he was seeing. The area was surrounded by what looked like metal panels and a lot of activities were going on inside. Heavy trucks were going in and coming out of the area. And he was able to spot a person inside wearing a hazard suit. *Hmm, what was on the train that required extra caution with the clean up? Weren't they overreacting!* he thought to himself. But anyway, who was he to know what the proper protocol was in major cases such as this. And the news was not giving any other details about the accident or what was on the train at that time.

Whether it was minor or considered a major disaster in a small quiet town of Oakland, Minnesota, nobody knew and no one was telling the whole story.

Deciding to stop his reconnaissance before he got busted, he left the woods and was back in time for dinner and to check on his guests.

Dinner was already at the kitchen table when he got home and Zian was putting the third glass for the third plate. Thea then came of out the kitchen and said, "I hope you don't mind that I went through the canned meat in your pantry. I wanted to call you but..."

He cut her off and said "No problem. It was good that you did. Zian must be hungry by now." He glanced at the boy who was now focused on watching television and still didn't show any reaction.

At the dinner table, there was an awkward silence in the air while they were eating, yet it was a good feeling for Eric because it had been a long time since he had dinner with companions. And he kind of liked it.

So, the next thing that came out of his mouth was, "You're welcome to stay here until you can afford to get your own place. If you need help looking for a job just let me know and I'll help in any way I can, maybe prepare your resume or get any necessary things you will need."

At that moment Zian looked him in the eye for the first time. He smiled and uttered the first word since their meeting, "Thanks!"

That broke the ice between them, and Thea started to share her experience from a previous work, "I was a waitress at a food and spirits restaurant. But I left after four months because some punks really knew how to ruin a good day. Alcohol was not for the people with weak mind and poor character. The combination would bring the devil at the table, and that's what I met the night I was fired."

– 0 –

Summer 1970, New Mexico

After putting baby Zian to bed, Thea routinely left

home at 7:30 pm to wait at the bar where she worked. This was the job that she could do without sacrificing the care of her son. Jane, a friend of hers, was usually left with the boy.

One night a group of five men came to the bar and sat at one of the tables assigned to her. It looked like they already had been drinking before coming to the bar. They were loud and looking red in their faces from alcohol consumption and starting to give her a hard time with their orders.

Suddenly the closest guy on her left grabbed her forearm and pulled her down toward him and said, "I think I got the house special already!"

Thea possessed an angelic beauty that was often mistaken as easy going and forgiving.

The group burst into laughter, and then Thea said back to him, "Sorry, but this house special isn't on the menu."

The guy holding her quickly pulled his hand off her like he just touched a pot of boiling water. The other men laughed again but this time at their friend. It turned out he didn't take rejection too well so he had to show that he was tougher. He stood up and was about to grab her by the upper arm when suddenly all the lights went off. Thea took that chance to defend herself from getting attacked so she grabbed his hand and twisted it hard, not to break it but just impair him. The lights turned back on after less than a minute. And that was when the other guys saw their tough friend seated back on his chair in pain while holding his one hand.

Thea stepped back, turned around and started to walk away when the guy in pain commanded, "Don't just sit there, you donkeys! Get her back!"

One guy stood up, gave chase, and grabbed her by the shoulder and said, "We're not done ordering!"

She turned around and her face radiated a very bright white light that temporarily blinded the men. She then landed a kick on the man's shin. The next thing the other men saw was their friend crawled on the floor holding his leg, in pain. The third man jumped on her but she happened to raise her elbow in time for his face to land on it. And the two other men just froze in shock if not in fear.

Thea reported that it was all a big misunderstanding, but the mess didn't sit well with her boss. The men were given free meal coupons for the mistreatment.

Thea confided that after she hog-tied the men with table cloth napkins, what she did was justifiable and she deserved to get paid if not rewarded.

Eric didn't know if she was joking with the hog-tie part but he still felt sorry for her and knew that waiting tables was not on the list of her job interests right now. He guessed it wasn't safe for her or maybe for the customers who might mess with her.

"Also, there's a school just a block away from here that you might want to check for Zian," he suggested. "He still can get in since school just started a couple of weeks ago. I think you should start with the school first so he won't be behind too much."

"Thanks. I'll do that first thing tomorrow morning," she agreed. "And thank you again, for letting us stay for a while."

That night, while changing, Eric saw that the back of his shirt had a tear. He forgot already that he got scratched while ducking his way under the wire. So he checked his back immediately and it turned out that there wasn't really any cut on his skin. His shirt had small blood stain on the ripped area but he just ignored it and threw the shirt into the trash can.

The next day, as he was getting ready for work that morning, only then everything started to sink in. It wasn't in his routine to pray before heading out the door but it was all changed. And, as he was in the middle of his prayer asking for protection, not to mention a less action packed day, his phone rang. It was Anne.

She was panicking because David had not come home, nor had he even called since the accident. He was about to offer to go to the authorities to report her husband missing when...

"Oh! Thank goodness he's here!" declared Anne.

"That's great! How is he?" asked Eric.

Rushing to hang up, she replied, "I'm sorry Eric, I'll talk to you later."

"Sure," he said.

After 30 minutes, his phone rang again. This time it was David. "Eric, I need your help. We need to see you!"

"Sure, I'll come over after work," he replied.

"It's really urgent and you need to come over

now. Please!!!" David begged.

He checked the time, it was only eight in the morning. He had an hour to spare before heading to work so he agreed to see them.

That day, as a result of train accident, the last four stations of the transit were closed temporarily. Using personal cars every day to work pained the commuters financially. People still experienced sluggish recovery from the catastrophic global economic recession five years ago. With the high gas prices, a majority of the working class preferred to commute by train rather than drive or even own a car.

When he got to David's place, he saw a couple of bags lined up by the door. He noticed Anne's eyes were still red and bit swollen from crying. He assumed that she was that overjoyed for her husband's return. But David looked more like tense.

After David offered him a seat, Anne went into the bedroom, maybe to attend to the baby.

"You look great. I was unsure, I thought you were badly injured during the accident," he said, happy to see the man who couldn't move even a finger a few days ago.

"Eric, there was more to the accident than what we think," David started saying. "Those people who rescued us worked for a big corporation named 'TriXGen'. They claimed that they handle the safety and security in the area of the crash. So, they did some tests on all of us at this clinic, which I couldn't identify. They took blood from all of us. And they did full body scans, too, after which we had to wait for the results before they would let us go."

"Did they say what was on the train that could pose a potential hazard to your health?" he asked out of concern.

"No!" David exclaimed in frustration over the unknown.

"After a day, they got the results and told us that they needed to do more advanced testing and close monitoring. They didn't even allow us to make phone calls. Then, they threw this bible-thick non-disclosure agreement in front of us. They told us that there's a place dedicated for us that is more equipped, more advanced, and can accommodate our families with us. They will provide everything we need, from jobs and houses to education for the kids."

Eric had no clues where David was going with his story and why he was there. The offer sounded great and it seemed that they didn't need any help from him.

Then David continued, "It's too good and happening too fast. I or we don't need their help in any means. Why can't we just go to a hospital of our choice and get the care that we want? Why move when we like what we have here? And what do we have that they need to monitor closely and discreetly? They weren't telling anything about us but more about the treasure waiting at the end of the rainbow in an unpleasant way. That was when I declined the offer. Then they took me to another room where they threatened me. The bigger guy told me straight that I have to do it or lose everything including my wife. It seemed like in a matter of one day they already know a lot about me.

"I was very worried that Anne was in danger at that time and with her condition I signed the contract. They told me that I'm not supposed to tell anybody not even relatives or friends about the move. They were successful at intimidating all of us and made us go along with it. Whoever's behind this is really evil. And I'm not going to drag my family down there."

At that point, Eric had to ask one thing that was bothering him, "Do they know that I was on the train too?"

"No. And I want to keep it that way," David assured him.

"How then can I help?" he asked.

David, sitting in an armchair next to the sofa where Eric was seated, leaned forward then clasped his hands. "Please take Anne and baby Emily right now and help them get a place away from here. I withdrew all our savings before coming home. Anne will be okay for a fair amount of time," David said, like praying for Eric to consider.

"But…what about Anne? Is she fine with it?" Eric asked, concerned about her current condition.

"As much as she wanted for all of us to just run away, it's dangerous and they might have followed me and be sitting outside the building right at this moment. If I take them with me, there's no guarantee that it will be safe where the TriXGen will take us. But one thing is for sure, they are not looking for you. Also, they only mentioned my wife but not my baby. You, Anne and the baby can walk out of here in plain sight and they will not even care. I beg you Eric, please help my family," David said in earnest.

Eric leaned forward and said, "Don't worry,

I'll do the best I can to keep them safe."

Anne came out of the bedroom with baby Emily wrapped comfortably in a cloth. David walked up to them and gave her a tender kiss on the forehead. Then he hugged her and the baby like it would be his last time to see them.

"They gave me until tomorrow morning to be back with her. I'll make something up for why she's not with me, and then maybe they will just accept it or worse look for her. If you leave now, my family will have enough head start to get far away," David said with hoarseness in his voice like he was trying to hold his emotion.

David then faced Anne and said, "I love you and I promise that I will see you and Emily again." Then he bent slightly down and gave baby Emily a kiss on the forehead and whispered, "We're doing this for you, I love you."

Eric grabbed the tote bags and said to Anne, "I'm sorry but we need to go now." He gently held her arm to slowly pull her away from her husband. David let go and turned his back on them; and that was when Eric saw that tears were running down his face.

With a baseball hat and sunglasses, she was

unrecognizable. And as David had predicted, they walked out of the building and straight to his car without any problem.

Eric immediately drove away and when he thought that they were in a safe distance away from the watch dogs, he called his office to let them know that he couldn't come in to work for personal reasons.

They drove south on highway 35 for five hours until they agreed that Madison, Wisconsin was a good place for her and the baby to live a quiet life. Also the distance was manageable for him to offer his time every other week to check on them or whenever they needed his help. They chose an apartment that was within walking distance of a supermarket, and they requested a unit on the first floor. All the transactions were under Eric's name so Anne would not be traced. And right after the mother and daughter settled in their new place, Eric left, promising to come back the next night to bring some necessities.

CHAPTER 5

Quiet on the Surface

Days passed without any hiccups in Eric's everyday routine. Thea landed a job at the nearest supermarket about 20 minute walk from their place. Zian advanced to fourth grade at Hugger Elementary School. It turned out that he was a lot smarter than his age. Since Thea couldn't provide the required documents in such a short period of time to the school, Zian then was given all the necessary tests to find out what grade to place him. And not only did he pass all the tests, he scored nearly perfectly on them.

One Friday morning, as Eric was getting ready for work, he noticed that Zian was still in bed. It was unusual on a school day for Zian not to be up before him. Thea was usually gone by 6:30 am, so he went to check on the boy.

Eric knocked on the door and called out,

"Zian, it's time to get up." He didn't answer so Eric knocked again. The boy still didn't answer so he opened the door. He stuck his head in to see if Zian was inside, and he saw him sound asleep. The boy's head was facing away from the door and the blanket was pulled all the way up to his ear. Eric walked up quietly to the sleeping boy. As he was about to touch the boy's forehead to feel if he had fever, the boy suddenly grabbed his hand as if he was going to smother him in his sleep.

"What are you doing?" asked Zian who was still a bit dazed.

"I noticed that you weren't up yet so I came in to check on you. I didn't mean to scare you," Eric apologized.

"I'm not going to school today," the boy murmured under the sheet.

Zian was a boy of few words. He's quiet and yet so deep. He seemed to observe everything first around him, analyzed the situation then acted accordingly.

"Are you sick? Do you need anything? Medicine, maybe…" he didn't get to finish his questioning when the boy cut him off…

"I'll be fine after I get rested. I get this every

now and then, so don't worry about me," the boy said then turned on his side facing away from him.

Poor kid, he told to himself. *He must be having a hard time adjusting to the new school. I can't blame him if he wanted to get a break once in a while.*

— 𝑜 —

A Week Earlier

Zian loved everything about his new school except for this one group of boys giving another boy a hard time. During recess the kids got to go outside and most of the boys played soccer at the field. He noticed that there was a boy that just stood by the sideline and watched all the time. And once in a while this group of boys kicked the ball at him then laughed. He didn't do anything at first because he was trying to give that one boy a chance to guard himself if not kick the ball back at them. After a few of those incidents turned out the same way, he realized that the boy wasn't going to do anything about it. So he befriended the boy, named Marty.

"Why don't I see you playing in the field? And why do you let the other boys treat you that way?" he asked the boy.

"I have a health condition that prevents me from doing anything tiring. Standing up to them is not the issue for me; the problem is I may not last the fight if it will happen. That will break my parents' hearts and I don't want to put them through that," Marty explained.

Marty was a very sweet humble kid who spoke with wisdom of a man. His courage was undeniable in the hearts of the people he cared about.

One recess time, Zian decided to join his new friend and stand beside him at the sideline. Then it happened, one of the boys in the group kicked the ball aimed at his friend. This time Marty did something unexpected, he stopped the ball with his two hands an inch before it struck his face. Wind swirling around his entire body seemed to be controlling his actions. He brought the ball down on the ground right in front of his right foot then kicked it hard that it created a trail of strong wind on top of the mean boys' heads raising up their hair then…hit the goal. That left all the kids on the field impressed and cheering except for the group.

Marty was ecstatic and jumping like he just won a championship. What he didn't realize was now he wasn't on the sideline anymore but on the field that he had been avoiding and afraid to step on.

Zian thought that the soccer incident would stop the mean boys, but he was wrong. Thursday of that week at the cafeteria, Zian didn't feel good about those same boys gathering at the other end of the aisle where his friend Marty, holding a tray with food on it, was walking down to join him for lunch. So, he didn't take his sight off them and his friend.

The boys who find satisfaction at embarrassing his friend, started to walk towards Marty from the opposite direction. Then one of the boys walked ahead of the others. And as that boy lined up with his friend he extended his right foot causing Marty to trip. At that point backpacks mysteriously started sliding on the floor towards Marty then piled up in front of him in time to catch his fall. The tray landed on the closest table on the left and the food landed neatly arranged on it. As if that wasn't enough to bewilder everybody, the broccolis started flying towards the mean boys, chasing them out of the cafeteria. When Marty got to the table, he saw that Zian had fallen asleep with the right side of his head resting on the table, and thought his friend just missed all the action.

Of course, the teachers didn't take the kids' hyper retelling of the incident seriously. It had happened before that school officials were pranked by the kids.

~ 0 ~

"Okay, there's food at the table. If you need anything you can call me," Eric told the boy then left.

That day, he decided to come home early. Zian was in the living room watching TV. He looked up-beat and even happy now; and his face somehow lightened up when he saw Eric. He sat on the couch beside the boy and watched the show too. The boy reached for the TV remote and handed it to him and said, "I'm not really watching. I got bored and didn't have anybody to talk to a while ago."

Eric took the remote, turned the TV off and said, "Okay then, I'm here now and you can talk to me."

There was hesitation on his part. He shook his head and then asked, "What do you want to talk about?"

"Anything. Why don't we start with a question? You go first. You can ask me anything you want," he said encouraging the boy to speak up.

"You're living alone. Where's your family?" Zian surprised him with that delicate question.

"I lost my parents when I was seven. In their will, they wanted me to stay with my godmother. I don't have grandparents anymore and I'm the only child. My godmother was the next of kin. She was a very close family friend and I met her few times right before she entered the convent. I was astounded when she fought to have me despite of the restrictions attached to her vocation. And surprisingly, she won! They allowed me to come and live at the convent. Before I joined her, my friends told me that nuns were really serious, no-nonsense people. So I was really afraid at first when I got there. I scrubbed floors, fed chickens and cleaned pig pens to name a few of my tasks," Eric narrated.

"That must be hard work for you," the boy said.

"Not really. As a young adventurous boy I was back then, I found it more fun. They all treated me like their adopted son. Parents get serious when they need their children to listen and listen well. They are no-nonsense when it comes to their kids' well-being. I left the convent after I graduated from high school. I worked to pay for my college. And I think...I can safely say that I turned out okay. What do you think?" he jokingly asked Zian.

"Yeah, you're a good person but lousy with grocery stocks. I didn't find any junk food in your pantry a while ago when I got hungry, not even a tiny packet of popcorn," the boy teased.

That made Eric laugh. It was his turn to ask the boy a question when Thea arrived. "I guess it will be my turn next time to ask a question," he told him. He stood up, rubbed Zian's head then went to his room to change.

The cleanup at the accident site was taking a lot longer than everybody expected. And that caused a group of concerned citizens in the community to complain and complain a lot to the point of bringing it up to the city officials. It turned out that the local officials were more upset about it because they were blocked from getting involved with the cleanup. It looked like a big private corporation with the blessing of the high federal agency was running it. One of the town officials who was able to initially check the area, leaked that there was a movement on the ground which created a 10 feet in diameter and 6 feet deep depression in the ground where a portion of it was right below the tracks that caused the train to derail. Maybe a fault line or sinkhole caused it, he guessed. That made the community panic and became very concerned about their property.

To calm the public, the transit company and the state put up a new temporary train route to eliminate the inconvenience and grievances. They sent out word that it was an isolated case that had been controlled and now was being taken care of. That brought the normalcy of the commute back like it was before. The protesting group then laid low.

CHAPTER 6

The Tourists

The following month, Eric thought it was time for him to take Thea and Zian for a little tour in town.

On their way to the city, the traffic suddenly came into a halt. Some people got out of their cars to see what was going on. When he saw the look of shocks in their faces, he hopped out of the car and looked to the direction of their concern.

A car ahead of them was on fire. He told his two passengers, "Wait in the car. I'll just see what's going on."

"Can I come?" asked Zian.

"No!" Thea and Eric both objected.

Eric walked zigzagging through the people standing beside their cars, and when he saw the blaze was getting bigger and wider at the front of the burning car, he started to run towards it. He stopped a couple of feet from the driver's side and looked through the window for any passengers inside. The inside was obscured by smoke and it was getting too hot around the car for him to stay long. He took off his shirt and covered his hands with it. He reached for the handle of the driver's door and opened it. That was when he saw a woman driver slumped on the steering wheel unconscious and restrained by the seatbelt. He held his breath and worked to free the woman from her seatbelt. He reached down to her right side and successfully unlocked the seatbelt in a matter of seconds. He wrapped his arms around her from behind passing under her arms. Then he quickly pulled her out of the driver's seat and carried her 35 feet away from the car. He laid her on the ground and started giving her CPR by compressing on the middle of her chest. After more than ten compressions, she started to cough. She still couldn't speak from coughing so Eric slowly raised the woman's upper body so she could cough better. She started pointing hysterically at her car repeatedly but he couldn't understand what she was trying to say. Did she want him to put the fire out, get her purse or something far more precious than those that she needed to get back so badly? He didn't think any of them he could possibly do because the car was engulfed in fire and it was just a matter of seconds before something bad and loud could really happen. The moment she could speak, she uttered the most terrifying thing Eric had heard in his life, "My baby is still in the backseat!"

He ran, and ran fast. He stopped ten feet from the car to pick up his shirt on the ground to protect his hands from the hot door handle, but that was when the car blew up.

He was thrown back and his ears rang. It felt like he was just hit by a wrecking ball.

He looked at the woman he just pulled out of that car and she screamed the most heartbreaking word that no person would want to say or hear in that kind of circumstance.

"Noooooooooo!" she cried out loud with her hands up in front of her like she would have rather stayed in the car than survived the horror of watching it explode with her child inside.

She pushed herself up, ran hysterically sobbing towards the burning car but Eric was able to grab her and hugged her tight to prevent her from getting hurt. They were too late.

After the explosion, they saw a shadowy figure coming out of the smoke a few yards away behind the car. It was Zian! He was holding a baby in his arms. The moment the woman realized who the boy was carrying, she shouted, "My baby!"

And that was when Eric let go of her and she ran towards Zian and took her baby.

Thea who was sitting in the front passenger seat didn't notice that her son had snuck out to the scene of accident. When she looked back to check on him, he wasn't there! So she jumped out of the car and ran towards where the explosion happened. She saw her son standing close to the smoking car not even realizing what the boy just did. Thea ran to Zian, she bent lower to speak closer to the boy's face while holding on to his arms then asked with tremendous panic in her voice, "Are you okay?"

"I'm fine," the boy answered.

She reached for her son's hand and walked him back to the car.

Then police cars started to arrive. Eric saw the woman run towards the policemen and that was when he walked back to his car while putting his shirt back on.

As he was sitting in the driver's seat waiting for the traffic to move, he looked at Zian through his rear mirror, who was seated in the backseat. They locked eyes for a few seconds then the boy looked away. Eric didn't want him to get in trouble with his mother so he didn't say anything about the boy's heroic action but at the same time putting himself in danger.

They arrived in time at the terminal for the next scheduled ferry that would take them to see the city's attractions by the river. So Eric bought the tickets in a hurry and they got on board. During the trip, Thea went to the restroom and he took the chance to talk to Zian about the recent incident.

"That was brave of you to do that," he told the boy.

"Just lucky I got there in time," the boy countered back.

"You're a great kid! You and your mother are lucky to have each other," Eric said.

"I guess now we're lucky to have you," the boy said smiling at him.

Eric saw Thea was coming so he ended their conversation by rubbing the boy's head.

"Mom, you need to call Jane," Zian told his mother.

Thea's face changed and looked so concerned.

"Is everything okay?" Eric asked them.

Thea then said, "I need to find a phone."

She went to the lower level where the snack bar was located and asked the woman behind it, "Can I please use a phone? It's an emergency."

The woman behind the counter told her that they don't have a phone there but she could talk to the Captain on the top deck.

They all went up to the Captain's quarters. Thea knocked on the glass section of the door and that got the Captain's attention. He opened the door and she didn't waste any time and spoke straight away, "Please! I need to place a call to New Mexico. It's an emergency."

The Captain complied easily and directed her to where the phone was.

She dialed the number and stayed on the phone for a while. Then she dialed again. She tried a few times to get through but didn't get any luck.

"Jane wasn't answering," she said in a sad tone.

They thanked the Captain then left.

While they were seated on the deck, Eric asked the second time, "Is everything okay? Who's Jane?"

She's a very dear friend. She's like family. We don't know if everything is fine with her," replied Thea.

She then got off the high chair, stood close beside Zian and placed her arm around him for comfort.

The rest of the trip was spent in deep thought and blank stares into nowhere for the three of them. Eric wasn't sure if his two companions even noticed the beauty of the city's skyline.

The next day, after he came home from work, he invited the boy for an ice cream in old downtown. The old downtown had interesting architecture. Most buildings were old but well maintained to keep their identity. The new ones were painted in bright contrasting colors to break the monotony of its nature. And the hilly grounds added authenticity to its historical beauty and serenity.

Since Thea would be staying a little bit late at work, he left a note on the kitchen table telling her where they went.

When they reached the ice cream parlor, it was packed with people, mostly kids. Some were already waiting in line outside the store. It looked more like a festivity where families were just scattered everywhere.

While waiting in line outside the parlor, Zian took the time to enjoy watching the cars on the main street right by where they were. It was a one-way street and the parlor was located on the corner of an intersection at the bottom of the road. When he followed the road going up to his left, he noticed a cylindrical truck on the uphill side swerving. It was coming down the road at a speed beyond the allowable limit. The boy looked back down at the traffic light which was on yellow for a moment then turned red. The first two cars at the light had a teenage boy driver with headphones and grooving to some music in one; and the close one to them had an older man driver. The car behind the teenage boy was a family van with a woman talking on a cellphone.

"Eric, the tanker over there!" Zian pointing to the direction of the truck, this time coming down honking and out of control.

Upon spotting the flame picture on its side and the word Petrol next to it, Eric instructed Zian to go inside the store and take cover. Then he darted towards the cars waiting for the light to change.

He waved his hands frantically at the side of the road to get the attention of the three drivers while shouting, "Clear the way! Move your cars! The truck is about to crash behind you!"

He instead got mean stares from them like he was a crazy guy. The teenage boy even locked his doors. Finally the old man in the car closest to him looked in his rear mirror and saw the truck reeling from side to side. He immediately took a right turn on the intersection and cutting the cars honking loudly and repeatedly.

Then Eric walked closer to the van and yelled at the woman, "Move your car now!" then pointed behind her, "that truck is out of control and will crash right at you!"

Strangely, a strong wind came out of nowhere and was pushing against the front of the tanker but not strong enough to stop it, only slow it a bit. But that was enough to buy Eric some time to clear the road at the bottom.

The grownups were grabbing their children and clearing out the area.

The woman in the van looked over her right shoulder and saw what was coming down the road. The tanker's honking was a lot louder and closer to warn everyone at the bottom of the road. Yet the teenage boy was still moving his head up and down to the music.

The van moved, and in panic bumped the car in front. The boy, feeling the whiplash from the bump, immediately removed his headphones, turned his engine off then got out of his car and chased the van he thought was trying to run away from him leaving his car behind.

Without wasting any time, Eric jumped in the car. But the tanker was at the bottom of the road closing in on him. Luckily the traffic light was green and the cars on the crossing road were stopped. He started to inch the car in an angle to move it to the left side when the tanker hit it from behind slicing off its side. The right half side of the car was dragged in the front of the truck while the other half where Eric was seated spun twice then stopped. The tanker settled on the other side at the bottom of the uphill road.

Fortunately, Eric was saved by his tight grip on the steering wheel and the air bag. He immediately ran back to Zian. The boy was seated slumped on the ground his back leaning against the full glass window of the ice cream store.

"I'm so sorry to just leave you like that," apologized Eric while hugging the boy. But something pulled him back…

"You feel hot! Are you okay?"

Then the boy passed out in his arms.

Thea opened the door for them and was surprised to see him carrying Zian, who was still out of it. "What happened?" she asked a little shaken.

"I'm so sorry! I think he's running a high fever," he answered while taking the boy to his bedroom. "He was fine when we left but…" Thea cut him off.

"Were you in trouble?" she asked.

"Well, not exactly. There was an incident downtown, but nothing bad happened," he answered.

But feeling guilty about leaving the boy he admitted, "But I left him for a few minutes trying to prevent a disaster on the street. I'm really sorry for having to leave his side."

"I think he'll be alright. He needs to rest," she said calmly.

CHAPTER 7

Not Normal Like Others

Part 1

Four months later, November 1990, Thea was doing so well at work that they were able to afford to move out and rent the unit across from Eric, right after the tenant vacated it.

"Can I still come over to your place?" Zian asked Eric, feeling sad that Eric wouldn't be a regular presence in his life.

"I'll be disappointed if you don't, especially when you get new additions to your toy planes," he replied then left to give them moment to enjoy their new space.

A week had passed when Eric was coming out of his apartment and he chanced upon a man and a woman with a little girl about seven years old in a wheel chair, and they were coming in his direction on the hallway. He pretty much knew every occupant on his floor and they were not familiar to him. He walked by them and while inching his body closer to the wall to give them more space to go by, he glanced at the little girl. She had this shy friendly smile that somehow brightened her aura despite the condition she was in. She had beautiful round eyes, pale skin, lips a bit dry, and wearing a bandana on her head to hide her baldness. That instant, it came to him that the woman was Sally, Thea's co-worker at the supermarket where she worked, and he greeted, "Hi Sally, how are you?"

"I'm fine. We're here to see Thea. This is my daughter Sam and my husband Johnny," replied Sally.

"Nice to meet you," Eric said to Johnny with a handshake.

Johnny tried to smile back but his eyes reflected deep sadness.

"See you guys around," he bid to them and went on his way.

It was nice that Thea and Zian were starting to entertain some friends, he thought. The visits from Sally and family became a pattern for a few weeks, and then just stopped. It was obvious to him that the little girl was sick, maybe she got worse, and they couldn't come to visit Thea anymore. He knew she must be devastated, so he went to check on them.

Eric knocked on the door and Thea opened. They walked up to the family room where she was entertaining a couple in their 70's and the woman just wiped the tears off her face while the man was comforting her.

"Oh! I can come back later," he said and about to turn around when…

"No, we're leaving anyway," the man said. And they thanked Thea for seeing them.

After the couple left, he asked in a nosey way, "Who are they?"

"I don't really know them. Somebody told them that I'm someone who could help a friend of theirs. But I told them that they got the wrong person. Anyway, what brought you here?" she asked.

"Just checking on you guys, and maybe we can all go out for lunch. My treat," he invited.

"Good timing. I got occupied by the couple and didn't have time to make anything. I'll get Zian," she said.

The entire time outside, the two showed no signs of sadness and neither spoke of any worries. So, he thought that there was nothing for him to fuss about.

Then a week passed and another set of guests appeared at her doorstep.

This time, a father and a son came out of her apartment. The father was holding onto the son, in his teens, and it looked like the boy needed guidance to walk and was having some difficulty talking. Same thing happened. There were regular visits from them and then stopped after a few weeks.

Coincidence? Maybe, Eric thought to himself. *But if it happens that a third visitor comes in under the same circumstances then there's something going on in there and I will find out what it is.*

Eric was at the end of the hallway walking up to his apartment when a man just entered Thea's apartment with a child on his arm. The child looked really malnourished, weakly resting her head on her father's shoulder.

Determined not to pass this one, he decided to ask Thea about it once the guests left.

Inside Thea's apartment, the father was trying to make Thea understand the condition of what his daughter was in.

"We've been to a lot of doctors across the country and all of them said the same thing. First they thought it was Crohn's but after bouts of treatments she'd feel better then it comes back again and again and now her body is not responding to any of the treatments. They can't find any cure for it. Nicky has been suffering a long time and she's losing the battle physically. She keeps telling us she's okay. But her mother and I know she is trying her best not to show her pain, not to make us sad. We are the ones not holding up well. She's still thinking of us even though she's the one hurting," said the father.

Thea then said, "I'm not here to take over anybody's place. I only come in when all help has been sought and nothing else is available. And I don't do it when there's no time left to spare. You can come back again next weekend and we'll start with the session."

The father then hugged his daughter tightly then sobbed not of desperation but happiness that there's another hope for his daughter to get better.

That night, Eric was about to knock at their door when he suddenly had a second thought. It wasn't his business anymore whatever was going on behind that door so he retreated back to his apartment.

The Sunday of the following weekend, the same guests arrived at Thea's apartment, this time the mother came along. Thea asked the couple to wait in the living room while she took the girl to the bedroom. Zian went with them to assist his mother. After a few minutes, the couple's attention was drawn to the bright light that shone through the gap between the bedroom door and the floor. And it so happened that Eric was walking outside the apartment building and his eyes were fixed at a window of an apartment which was illuminated by that very same bright white light. Then it came to him that it was coming from Thea's apartment unit.

The incident disturbed him enough to have the courage the next day to talk to Thea about what he had been observing for the past couple of months. So, he knocked on the door across his and Thea opened on him. "You're just in time, dinner is served. Please join us!" she invited.

Eating with them had been the tradition whenever he was around. He even had their permission to go through their refrigerator whenever he came home from work and didn't have time to prepare a meal.

After dinner, the boy invited him to check out his new military toy planes. Then, after a while he excused himself to the boy for he needed to talk to his mother. So he proceeded to the kitchen where Thea was cleaning up. "Oh, Eric do you need anything?" she asked upon seeing him.

He walked around the dining table, rested his hands on top of a chair's backrest ready to get straight with her. "Well, I noticed some people coming in and out of here. And one thing common in them was someone looking not so well. If you don't mind me asking, what was going on?" he asked, his face firmly focused on hers, waiting for a sincere answer.

Thea instructed him to sit then she poured him a cup of tea. She sat across the table to him and got herself her own cup then started out by asking, "Can you promise that whatever I tell you right now will stay in this room regardless of whether you believe me or not?"

"Yes," promised Eric.

CHAPTER 8

Not Normal Like Others
Part 2

Thea studied Eric for a while, then began her story, "I'm from another world called Gaulkan. We arrived here 1969 aboard a special vehicle we called Morsel. It was shot down and crashed in Albuquerque, New Mexico."

Eric slightly tilted his head for a second as if having a hard time understanding what he just heard.

"You said *we*? Aside from you and Zian, are there more out there right now?" he asked.

"Right before we reached our target site, my guide, Usil, who was piloting, detected at some distance ahead that the ground was filled with people and activities. He identified a few heavy machines aimed straight up in the sky crossing our path ahead. He made a wise decision to release the pod I was in right into the first deep lake that he found."

At this point Eric had to stop and asked, "Wait, please be patient with me, I need to make sure I'm following you correctly. Are you human like me?"

"I am human in my world. But crossing to your world changed my being. I cannot die here. I'm immortal here. I can only die in my world," she answered.

Somehow Eric relaxed if not dumbfounded by her explanation and gave a nod of acceptance.

Thea then continued on, "Usil, my pilot, made a brave move to proceed to the site to divert the attention away from my location. He went down with the Morsel. He was my husband's trusted friend and supporter. He was supposed to be my guide and protector here. We will always be grateful to him for saving me and sacrificing himself."

Thea managed to hold back the tears in her eyes and took a sip of her tea.

Eric took the chance to ask, "So, did you find out what happened to your friend?"

"No," Thea said while shaking her head.

"What happened then after you were

dropped?" Eric asked.

"I was able to swim to the shore. And as I walked towards the dry ground, a child happened to be there and saw me. He stood still, frozen, stunned either to see me coming out of the water from nowhere or because of my odd clothing. I was dressed in full shiny silver colored outfit from head to toe. It was a special kind of metal fabric that was light and yet tough enough to protect me from getting punctured by sharp objects. It was stylishly superior where I came from but I think it was a little bizarre fashion for a normal person here. I walked up to him and told him that I swam the wrong way and got lost. Then I knew he's mesmerized by what I was wearing so I made a deal with him. I asked him to find me some clothing and in exchange I would give him my metallic outfit that is fit for a queen. The boy ran as fast as he could to the back of a house and then reappeared in a few minutes with a shirt and pants that looked more like his father's clothing. I asked him to turn around while I changed and then I handed him my clothes. He smiled and ran back to the house again and that was my chance to run away, too, before he told on me."

"Why here?" Eric asked out of curiosity.

"Why not," answered Thea. "You shelter the

homeless generously! And that's exactly what I came here . . . *for REFUGE*.

Eric wondered and asked, "How did you know a lot about us?"

Thea paused, and in a mild tone replied, "We've been gathering data about your world for hundreds of years and studying them. Prior to my arrival, I was well-equipped with knowledge of how to adapt here.

"And my first stop, of course, was a homeless shelter. Don't you know that Albuquerque, New Mexico has fair number of them? It didn't take me long to find one. And that was where I met Jane."

Just then Zian appeared in the kitchen with eyes all droopy.

"Hi, buddy!" Eric greeted the boy.

"Mom, I'm going to bed now," Zian said to his mother.

"Alright. Brush your teeth first," she instructed her son.

"I did already!" the boy replied while walking away.

"Speaking of Zian, why weren't you mentioning him in your story?" Eric asked.

There was a long silence before she answered, "I was pregnant with him."

He was taken aback with what he heard. To get some clarity he asked, "You said that year was 1969. If you were pregnant with Zian, then he should be in his 20's by now. But he's still a young boy?!"

"He looks young because we aged slowly," she answered, "and that was one of the reasons why the leader of our world created a law that every family will only have one child. If it happens that another one comes along then he can take the older one for his soldier and be a part of his dominion. If the family doesn't comply, he orders his army to take the child by force.

"He trains them to worship him. They are not allowed to leave the place even to see their families. And that is how it would be till the day they die. It was a verdict that can never be reversed. We never realized how it felt for other families to go through it until we found out I was pregnant with Zian. Am I boring you now?" Thea asked, making sure Eric wasn't asleep with his eyes open.

"Are you kidding me? I'm so rattled right now that my mind even rejects the thought of sleeping. Trust me, nothing you just revealed bored me a bit," Eric assured her.

"My husband and I decided for me to leave because our world is not safe anymore for our sons and daughters, and for the next generations," Thea added.

"Why didn't your entire family leave?" asked Eric. He was struggling to make sense of the decision that split the family.

Thea looked him in the eye and asked, "Did you ever ask yourself what your purpose in life is; and if you are on the right path of achieving it? It better be one that is noble. Or better yet one that will leave a positive impact to any child."

Eric just gulped in response.

To answer Eric, she continued, "My husband, with my first son, organized a group that unites the families victimized, those who will be victimized, and individuals who believe that Gaulleo's reign must end. It's time for us to stand up to him. He's not going to make another family one child less. And my husband wants to make sure that it will be done.

"We planned to come here without creating any troubles but the hostility that greeted us forced me to go into hiding."

"Where did you stay prior here?" asked Eric.

"I first met Jane at the shelter. She was in her 70's and worked as a cook getting less than minimum wage. She didn't do it for the money. She was living alone and trying to keep herself busy at the same time having a social life. We became good friends and the shelter had been our social club. When she found out that I was pregnant, she offered to let me stay at her place since the shelter was a little inconvenient for me to have a child," said Thea.

"Anyway, it's getting late, so to cut the story short we are not like you. The power within us that was being suppressed in our world works here. We have abilities to do things beyond human limits. Anything that exists has its circuitry that we are capable of tapping and altering. And that's what I've been doing with the sick children. I made them well. One thing I don't do is to come in when it's the dying moment. I could mess up the order that is adequately shielding your world. God has a way to keep the balance in everything between the three worlds. A human soul leaves the body even before the last breath is taken. If I help at the time the soul is outside, there's a big chance another soul will take over and the person will not be the same person anymore. Worse, it could open a door for the dark world to come in. On the lighter note, I can also produce heat; from the smallest amount for simply boiling a pot of water to a lightning temperature that can turn anything around me to ashes."

Thea ended her story with a request, "Please don't give us up. We don't have any plan of causing troubles. And we will leave in peace when it's time."

"What about Zian? What can he do?" asked Eric.

"Zian is a special boy. He is my opposite. But I don't encourage him at this point. He is still young and using his ability sometimes weakens him physically. He needs to learn to control the energy within him," Thea said.

"If you landed in New Mexico, then what brought you here to Oakland, Minnesota?" he asked.

"The Morsel that brought me here was kept somewhere at the area of the train site where you found us. We were in the process of locating it. When we get the message that it's safe to go back then that will be our ride home," she paused and release a sigh of disappointment. "But we lost the signal when the accident happened."

— ∂ —

Two days before the train accident in Oakland, Minnesota; Zian excitedly called out to his mother, "Mom! The rod! It's lighting up!"

Thea dropped what she was doing in the kitchen and ran to the bedroom where her son was staring at the flickering blue light inside of a silvery metallic glass rod, six inches long and one inch in diameter. It had a tiny round crystal fitted at one end. She couldn't believe what she was seeing. The boy then gently handed the rod to his mother.

She held on the rod with her right hand, having the fingertips of her four fingers and the thumb pressed on it with the crystal end pointing up. At that instant, a blue light shined out and an image of a map appeared showing a meteor-like vehicle located in the area of Oakland, Minnesota.

Zian knew that they were different and from another world. Thea had told him everything. He was aware of the sensitivity of the situation they were in and that it was necessary for them to keep their identities a secret in order to live at peace.

A trip up north was of utmost importance for Thea to take. So she talked to Zian about taking a short visit to Minnesota to find the Morsel.

The next day, with just a backpack to fill, they squeezed in necessary stuff such as cash, a toy plane, a couple of undergarments, and most important of all...the rod.

It was eight at night when they arrived at the Minnesota domestic airport. After grabbing dinner, Thea hailed a cab to take them to Oakland town. She had the map written down and instructed the driver to take them to a gas station north of the marked spot on her map where the Morsel was located. They got to the place around ten at night. She was shocked to see that the area was inhabited. They popped quickly inside the store of the gas station and bought a flashlight.

They stood outside the store for a few minutes to check the direction to take. They crossed the road then passed through the clear part of the field a bit to the right before the wooded area. It was a pitch-black night, the ample stars in the sky and the bright moonlight provided enough light to see their way. When they got deeper in the field, Thea took the rod out of the backpack and this time the blue light in the center of it was flickering faster and brighter.

"What's going on, Mom?" Zian asked, a little uncertain about what his mother was doing.

"Oh, the light will let us know when we locate the vehicle," she calmly answered. "It should stop flickering once we find it."

As they walked closer to the marked spot on her map, the flickering from the rod gets faster and faster. After taking a couple of steps, the light stopped flickering; but the ground underneath their feet started to shake. They stopped and stayed still to feel what was going on. The light from the rod suddenly went away. Then the ground started to break. Thea immediately stuck the rod in the rear pocket of her jeans. Zian grabbed her waist and she held him tightly. The ground they were standing on suddenly sunk and they were dropped down into a six feet deep hole. As they were slumped on the ground she heard a sound of a coming train then a light was shining above them. She stood up immediately then raised her son by grabbing around his upper legs. "Zian, reach the top and pull yourself up while I push you," she instructed, exhibiting that sudden gush of mighty strength a mother could experience when a child's in danger.

Her son was able to get to the surface, but she was still in the hole when the boy shouted, "Mom, hurry! The train is coming!"

Thea was having a hard time grabbing on to

something to get out. The train was closing in on the track with a portion of it suspended over the hole she was in.

"Go! Run!" she shouted back to her son.

Instead, the boy closed his eyes, then a strong wind pushing upward started to form underneath Thea's feet. Next, her whole body was being pushed up. As she was being raised out of the hole, she grabbed Zian by his two wrists. They were both thrown a few yards away when the train passed by. It went off the tracks, skidded, flipped on its side and then stopped. The last car crashed into the hole.

— 0 —

"That's why Zian looked so weak that time when I saw the two of you sitting in the grass," Eric said to Thea.

"I understand if you decide to distance yourself from us now. We wouldn't be offended. It might take a while for Zian to get used to it but he will in time," she said.

"I don't see any reason to stay away from you. Anyway, I'd better go back to my place. It's really late. Thanks again for the dinner," he said then left.

CHAPTER 9

Just When Things Get Better

Present Day, November 26, 2029

Since it will be a needle in a haystack to contact even one survivor after decades have passed, I'm left with one source that seems to know more than the short notes and broken clues that he is trying to drop my way like crumbs of bread.

All I need now is to have a serious chat with Shadow. And I know just how to do it. I let two weeks pass without doing anything about my ghost or my research. I don't think he just wants to orchestrate the entire investigation and let me do the work without gaining something out of it. He must have a personal purpose for helping me. And what could it be?

I know Shadow will get impatient sooner or later with fear of losing his pawn. So I'll just wait until he makes the contact. And the next time he does, I'll make sure it's going to be face to face.

Monday, December 10, as I suspected, someone stuck an envelope under my door with a crumpled piece of paper inside. I'm grinning when I read what is written on the paper, *Shadow wants to finally meet this coming weekend.*

Before I embark on this dangerous meeting with a stranger, I'm going to try to enjoy this week the best way I can.

On my way to work, I stop by at my coffee shop to grab a cup of my usual cappuccino. While standing in the line, a man behind me asks, "Excuse me, I found this dime on the floor by your foot. Is it yours?"

I check the thing he's holding and says, "No."

I glance quickly at him then turn to face front. Not letting the chance pass, he speaks to me again, "By the way, I'm Mark."

Not to be snobbish, I turn to face him and give him a timid smile.

"I often see you here, maybe you'll let me buy you a cup?" the guy offered, trying to be cute this time.

I always try not to show my over-excitement at anything that will expose my vulnerability, so I reply, "Thanks, but I got this one."

"Maybe a dinner, then?" he insists.

"I'll think about it," I say.

He hands me his card and says, "If you decide to accept my invitation just give me a call."

I've seen him a few times at the coffee shop but this is the first time I've seen him up close. He exudes a smooth confidence underneath his rugged look. Fair-skinned, long dark wavy hair stroked away from the face, almond eyes, thin lips, sweet smile, speaks in a manly low tone voice and dresses neatly. My guess is he's about six feet inches tall based on my height of five feet seven and a half inches. All checks in my 'yes, I like to get to know the guy' list.

"Sure," I reply while taking his card.

It is my turn to place an order, so I step forward to the counter. Two minutes later, they hand me my coffee then I walk out without even glancing at him, though I wish I did.

When I get to the office, my assistant is already waiting for me at the reception area and excitedly announces that a meeting has been called to announce something important. And based on what she heard from the grape vine, our team was chosen to handle our major client's next creative marketing. I'm supposed to be high-fiving her, instead I'm staring blankly at her and my mind is so busy assessing the events in these first hours of my day. Is this some kind of sign telling me not to go to my meeting with Shadow? Everything seems to be falling into place and it would be crazy for me to just throw all these away for something uncertain.

"Tally! Did you just hear what I said?" my assistant wakes up the consciousness in me.

"Oh, let's not get ahead of the situation here," I answer.

My assistant and I arrive at the meeting and she is right! It is announced that our presentation captured the client's heart. That night I'm feeling so blessed and overjoyed that I need to call Kate to share the highlights of my day. We talk for hours on the phone like always until we realize that it's past midnight. We regularly talk about everything under the sun. And talking about our day's events and pouring out our emotions over it help take a load of stress out of our heads. In a way, it's like therapy minus the therapist. And as always, she's more excited than I am about my new acquaintance.

Friday, I invite my parents to have dinner with me. While eating our meal, my father starts to talk with a serious tone in his voice, "Tally, your mom and I decided that it would better if we just sell the business and use the money to travel. We always dreamed of going to Rome. We want to do it while we are still strong and able to walk. You're welcome to come."

"But..." I'm about to object when my father calms me into accepting the inevitable...

"We're old and may not live to enjoy life at the fullest with all the problems we're dealing with at the diner, so it's final. You worried long enough about us that you neglected your own personal life, like having your own family," my father speaks with a look of concern in his face.

"Well, speaking of that, I met a guy who just asked me out," I say with the intention of assuring them that I have hope of achieving that aspect of my life.

"Good!" my father says with a hint of excitement.

I know my mother will not let this topic fizzle out without asking, "So when can we meet him?"

I explain to them that I don't really know the

guy yet but I will definitely bring him to meet them once I'm sure of what his real intention is.

My parents don't know how far I've gone to resolve their problem at the diner. I'm keeping it from them because I know they would rather lose the business than lose me in the process of solving it. Being parents doesn't stop when children move out of the house. They will always be on the sideline watching us while we play our games on the field. Every fall we make, they fall harder; and every pain we take, they grieve over it. What they don't sometimes realize is that it goes both ways. We feel the same way too. I will not let them give up the business because I know for sure it will break their hearts, so in the end, I decide to go with the meeting.

CHAPTER 10

I Meet my END

Sunday, December 16; the note from Shadow a week ago doesn't have a street number or street name. He gave one familiar landmark closest to his place but after that it looks like a treasure hunt where 'X' marks the spot. And in bold print, he wrote, "You must not tell anybody about this. Come alone."

I leave everything up to God. If this has a positive result then I'm grateful, but if not then I'll surrender everything up to Him.

I reach the entryway to Shadow's property. I can tell because of the dilapidated mailbox with...the red letter X painted on it. I then drive up the dirt road that passes through a wooded area with big old trees lined up the sides of the path that stretches about a quarter of a mile. I always tell myself not to ever fall for something or someone not bearing clean identification.

Now here I am standing right in front of the small stone house that looks like a big boulder, all by myself with only a maze to protect me. I also have my keys though, which I always have at hand whenever I walk to my car in any parking lot. I put them between my fingers, the tips pointing out, as my weapon that can impair anyone who gets a poke on the weak area under the eye.

Behind the house are all trees that wall the back of it as if trying to hide a wilderness where one can never get out alive and that made it a scarier place to be in. But what else is there to hang on but the closest one with the veracity of his accounts and maybe the only answer that will stop the ghost train from making more apparitions.

I ring the doorbell and shiver runs up my spine, not knowing what will appear at the door or if this is a psychotic hoax and I may not see tomorrow. When a boy opens the door, I feel a little relieved for I know no one would dare to do something awful in the presence of a boy. With that, I sense the blood flowing back to my face.

Before I get to introduce myself, the boy calls out, "Eric! She's here!"

The boy let me in and leads me to the living room. "Please take a seat. Can I get you anything?

Water?" he asks.

"No, thank you. I'm fine," I reply. But in the back of my mind I'm thinking of the worst case scenario where I drink the water and next thing you know I'm tied at the table, hooked up to every wire imaginable and ready to get operated on. Now, I feel like I'm not taking normal breaths.

The living room is a little under-furnished with only one long white leather sofa and one average size oval marble center table. The marble flooring blends well with the stone-tiled walls and wooden beams that spread across the entire ceiling of the room. Across the living room is a small kitchen with a round dining table fit for three chairs, and a few appliances. Above it is a mezzanine that seems to have a room which I find odd to have a stained glass window without any opening that is facing the living room where I am sitting. And I can't see any obvious stairs that go up to the mezzanine. There are two medieval looking wooden doors in the kitchen, which I assume are one for the bathroom and the other for storage.

To shake off the paranoia in my head, I strike up a conversation with the boy. "Are you Eric's son?" I ask.

The boy just smiles and says, "Eric will be

106

with you in a moment."

Then, one of the doors in the kitchen opens and a man walks out. "Thank you, Zian," he says to the boy, as the boy exits the same door.

I stand up and my mind is shouting to run for the door but my heart whispers to calm down and as the cliché goes -- he could be the one. He's approximately five feet ten inches tall, short dark brown hair, clean shaven, nicely tanned skin, hooded eyes, full lips, flashes a charming smile, dresses casually, and most of all walks with a cane so what's there to be scared of. But what do I know; sometimes psychos hide themselves behind their neat appearances.

I lock eyes with him for a long time. Then it feels like I've known him in the past.

"Hi! I'm Eric Neil Dutton," introducing himself, his left hand takes a hold of the cane then he raises his right hand for a handshake.

I shake his hand with a firm grip to let him know that I'm not going down without a fight.

"Please, sit down," he says. "Thank you for coming. I know it wasn't easy for you to accept my invitation but I assure you that you will leave this place without a scratch."

I give him a smirk, then say, "First, don't do that again. You can't just keep sneaking behind someone and dropping notes. It scared the life out of me. Second, don't send lousy directions when you invite a woman for a meeting. And third, I came here to get some answers and you better have some."

"First, sorry for giving you such distress. The notes were just to assure you that if in case you ran out of options then there was still someone left to talk to. Your second point, I'm working on it. Third, I have the answers that you wanted," he says.

"The area that your parents own is a fraction of the land that was known before as the 'Blackout Zone'. There was indeed a train accident that happened there in the year 1990. The land looked calm on the surface but underneath it concealed a big secret that held an important piece not belonging here on earth. They hid a valuable vehicle and its occupant with the desire to explore their origin and with that they worked on arming humans with equal if not more superior resources. In the process, there were innocent victims…that included me. You need to help me expose this organization and their reckless actions. Please, I really need your help."

"Why me?" I ask.

Eric then looks at me straight in the eye and

says, "I want to make sure that the person who will help me has a higher purpose in solving the problem at hand than selling me out."

"Then why not just do it yourself?" I counter.

"If they trace and capture me and everyone connected to me, then the truth will never get out. I'm living evidence of what is being done behind the walls of conspiracy that happened 39 years ago right at your parents' property. Now is the time to let the people know that they are vulnerable to treachery, abuse and manipulation by those in power who will do anything at all costs just to feed their inflated ambitions that go as far as out of this world," he says with strong conviction.

He sounds like he is ready to wage a war against the people who did something really bad to him. One thing for sure, he is not the one on the front line.

"What do you mean by 'they'?" I ask not following what he just said.

Before he answers, our attention goes to the same door where he came out. It opens and a woman in her late 40's walks out carrying some kind of thick book. She hands it to Eric and he says, "Thank you, Thea."

She smiles at me then retreats through the same door. In my attempt to get a description of what's behind the door, I half-jokingly say, "I see you have a party in there." But that falls on deaf ears.

"The TriXGen Corporation, the one I was referring to as 'they' a while ago, is a collaboration between a big private organization and the government," he continues.

He then hands me the book and says, "This is a copy of my journal. I recorded detailed events that led me to discover the truth. You can go through it when you get home."

"What made you think that I will help you after all the distress you've caused me, all the more my parents?" I ask in stern voice, reluctant to give in.

The casual look in his face turns serious. He pushes his hips as far back as they can go in the chair. He sits upright then takes a deep breath before speaking.

"That day put a curse on me. I will never be the same. The people I will love will come and go but I'm left here in a cycle that will hurt over and over again. I got infected by a substance that the TriXGen's top scientist developed. The source of it was the being they found inside the vehicle that came here from another world 60 years ago. Whatever that one had, I have now. It co-exists with my being," he says with a heavy heart.

I panic upon hearing that he's infected with something, so I immediately ask, "Wait, is what you have right now contagious like we're not supposed to be standing this close?"

"No, it's not contagious. But if you happen to feel something unpleasant inside of you any time just let me know," he says.

When he notices the look of disbelief in my face, he immediately takes back what he said, "I was just joking about the unpleasant feeling part."

"Ha! Not funny," I counter.

"I'm sorry. You're safe right now," he says.

"So how did you get infected?" I ask.

He then continues, "When the accident happened in the Blackout Zone, 39 years ago, on your parents' property to be exact, the bunker underneath it was used as TriXGen's secret lab. The area where the experiment was being conducted collapsed and some amount of substance spilt and somehow leaked through cracks in the ground and out in the surface of the accident. All survivors inhaled it, and got infected with it. Luckily the area wasn't inhabited, and it dissipated into the air."

"There are people out there like me who are suffering the consequences of the TriXGen's careless actions to feed its ambitions. The person on top of this is someone who wanted to add a fifth star on his shoulder if he succeeds in creating war between our world and another. And more will turn like me and will be placed in the fish tank if we don't stop them. The help I'm asking is not for me. I am who I am now and there's nothing anyone can do about it. But the people that are not affected yet can still be protected. And the others like me who have families are suffering too from separation, and they can be helped. I can't fight this alone but I'm not going to force you to help me."

"In case I decide to help, what do I need to do?" I ask, making sure I know what I'm getting into.

"Your best bet is the newspaper. You can keep your anonymity. Reporters are protected by law not to reveal their sources. Think about it and decide after you read my journal. Whatever you decide on, I guarantee you that the ghost train will stop bothering your parents' diner," he commits.

Eric exudes an integrity that I can't fool myself not to trust and believe in.

What I can't comprehend is not what happened in the past but what is in front of me at this moment. The man I'm talking to doesn't age at all. He looks about couple of years older than me.

CHAPTER 11

The Birth of a New Village

I leave Eric's place feeling overwhelmed by too many scenarios playing in my mind.

I get home at ten in the evening and I don't feel any hint of sleepiness. I place the journal on my bedside table. I grab a snack from the refrigerator, and no matter what I do, my mind is in the journal. I don't even need a cup of coffee to keep me awake, so I hit the shower then hop on my bed. I plan to read this journal as much as I can until my eyelids drop. I pick it up then prop it on a pillow resting on my lap. I carefully fast-scan through the first few pages and notice that most of the dates started way back in 1990. *This is going to be a long read*, I tell myself. I just hope that it will be interesting enough to keep me awake.

Who needs a time machine when you have Eric's journal.

It starts with June 1990 – The Train Accident, followed by Encounter with Thea and Zian, and then David Smith and Family. I start to doze off after those events.

The next night, I continue on where I left…

– ∅ –

Friday, November 1, 1991

The day of the dead marked the completion of the Oakland town train accident site clean-up. With that, the area was given a name "Blackout Zone" where trespassing and loitering were illegal. Signs were put up and hung on the barbed-wire fence that covered the accident site and its surrounding area.

But that didn't stop people from sneaking in, from curious little children to nosey grown-up teenagers. In a matter of weeks, a lot of arrests were made, though no jail time was warranted.

For a while the place was calm and not even a minor unlawful event happened, until one night. Three thugs decided to explore the area and check what they could take and sell for fast money. Based on the police report that was released to the public, the three were armed with a cutter and a flashlight and they cut a portion of the fence and easily went in. They kept walking eastward towards the center looking for any discarded materials when the men encountered a big black bear. All their experiences running away from the authorities paid off, and trained them really well to run like the wind, thus saving them from getting devoured.

The three then went straight to the local police station to report the incident.

But upon learning what the true intention of those men, the receiving officer locked them in for just a night.

The next day, two local authorities drove up to the Blackout Zone to investigate the report. They scoured the place but didn't find the bear or any evidence that one had been in the area. Regardless, they released a warning to the public to be alert and stay off the vicinity.

Unfortunately, it was followed by a tragic incident when a large number of teenagers stage a secret late night party in the area. A bloody ruckus ensued that sent one of them to the hospital fighting for dear life.

At the start of 1992, there was a growing number of reports and complaints from the community regarding the safety in the Blackout Zone. Therefore, the government decided to possess the 250 square mile desolated eastern side of Oakland town where the Blackout Zone was located. And with it sprouted a new village they named Silverlake, population 0. The temporary tracks constructed in Oakland side became the official route for train.

Woods and crops were removed. Lands were partitioned and sold to different private and public organizations. The Blackout Zone located on Circle Drive was the only one left unsold. Whether it was not put up for sale or nobody wanted a piece of land with a history of holes in the ground, it remained a vacant lot for years.

– 0 –

So, that's where the Silverlake is now! I excitedly utter to myself.

CHAPTER 12

The Silence

I never realized how much I'm captivated by Eric's journal. Even at work I can't wait to go home and continue with my reading.

− ø −

October 8, 1995 − Reconnected With David Smith

I received a call from David five years later. "Eric, it's David Smith. Remember me from the train accident?" the voice on the other line greeted.

The accident and all the events that

followed it were still fresh in my mind like they just happened yesterday, so I replied, "Of course! David, how are you?"

"Still surviving," he replied.

Since it was the first time that David successfully made a contact, he was in a rush to hang up the phone afraid to be caught, so he quickly asked, "How's my family?"

I told him that they were okay and safe. David thanked me and said he will call back again then hung up. I called Anne right away and told her that David just called but we didn't get the chance to talk longer.

"He just needed to know that you and Emily are doing fine," I told her.

She was ecstatic about the news. Any proof that her husband was alive was enough for her to hold on and hope that someday they could see him again. I promised Anne that I would call her once I heard from him again.

As I expected, David called again a week later and this time it was past midnight. David told me to purchase a prepaid phone dedicated to our line of communication and install the application 'OverAndOut'. The application was created by a geek teenage girl who didn't want her parents tracking her every move and monitoring her every chat. It would allow people exchange messages then get deleted permanently once closed after they were read. No records to be traced. David gave a number to send him a text message through the app after midnight once I accomplished everything.

After I agreed to it, he hung up.

I thought that for a while my life was back to normal, but then I realized that the accident was the start of what normal life was now for me and all I could do was to get used to it.

"I'm set. Waiting for your call," I texted.

But David didn't reply.

After two days, midnight of October 19, a call came in, "Eric, it's David. Are you okay to talk right now?"

"Yes, what happened to you? Are you okay? Where are you now?" I barraged him with questions I had wanted to ask the first time we talked.

David then started out by saying, "I'm doing fine but missing my family so much. They took me to this island up north, the farthest up on the US map which is surrounded by lake. They went this far to shut me up. It's extreme isolation. Once a month they place me in an incubation for a couple of hours. They call it cleansing procedure. My suspicion is that machine is trying to destroy something inside of me. I think they knew what I had right after the initial tests they did back there. I guess I have what the others here have. And that's what I'm going to find out. "

If it's just a lake, can't you take the risk to swim your way out of there? I thought of asking David.

But David continued on, "Others attempted to escape by swimming their way out but right when they saw the shore to freedom they were met with crocodiles. Imagine, infesting the lake with the most ferocious creatures on the planet! The water doesn't even freeze in winter! Who knows what else is out there even when you get lucky enough to get to the shore? And there's a tower that appears to be a lighthouse but everyone knows that it's like the Tower of Babel. Good thing one was able to swim back to tell the story when he saw the others getting attacked. It may not be how they wanted it to end but I guess anywhere but here that we call the 'fish tank' is a better place to be. The only thing holding me back from taking the dive is my family. How are they, by the way?"

It was all good things that I could say about his family and David was so elated to hear that Emily started kindergarten. Anne liked her job as a Nurse Assistant at a hospital and the hospital provided a child care service for all employees with little kids. That seemed to relieve him.

"What about the other survivors on the train?" I asked out of curiosity.

"They're all here. George, in his 70's, took his wife with him. San, a migrant from Thailand, cries a lot, and like me, is trying to hang on. And Ulysses, the bachelor in his 40's, took the move and isolation a lot easier," he replied.

"What about the train engineer?" I followed up since he didn't mention anything about him.

David gave a big sigh and said, "He works for them. They call him the Eagle. He monitored any disturbances on the surface above the bunker that time. And he was the one who reported the accident to TriXGen then took off immediately.

"I knew if I just held on long enough to gain their trust, then there's hope. I didn't think it would take this short time.

After five years, they've given me a position at the lab they call 'The Fort'. They knew that I'm a Mechanical Engineer by profession and that made it more convenient for me to get in. And right after a few weeks of working with the organization's top people, I found out that what we are working on is a copy of a vehicle they called the 'Capsule'. It's very advanced and special that all of them had never seen or heard about. My Lead Engineer let me in one time to see the real thing on the first ground level. It looked like two persons would be manning it. Also, there's one pod for safety escape but it seemed like another pod beside it was missing," David narrated.

"Do you know what it's for?" I asked.

David relayed what he heard so far, "The ones we are building will be used as vehicles to explore other possibilities beyond our world. But the Capsule that arrived at the Fort the same time we came to the island was not built on our world. And the occupants here thought we were the ones who brought it here. It turned out it was located previously at a 100 year old bunker 50 feet below the tracks where our train ran. The bunker was weakened by previous earthquakes with the strongest being 8.5 in magnitude. And at the time of the accident, one wing of the bunker caved in and caused the ground to sink and the train to derail."

"A bunker beneath the Blackout Zone!" I exclaimed. "No wonder it took a long time to clean up that place."

"Hold on...I hear someone outside my room, gotta go. I'll call you soon. Please tell Anne I love her," David whispered then hung up.

$- \mathbf{\theta} -$

My parents' property is sitting on top of contaminated land not to mention its historical foundation that could be a potential target for annihilation, I thought to myself. Heck, this journal is sucking the sense of reality out of my sleepy head!

I place a bookmark where I stop, put the journal down on the nightstand then go to sleep.

CHAPTER 13

The Secret Structure

Thursday, December 20, 2029; during my morning run to the coffee shop, I spot through the glass window a familiar face sitting at the small table right by the entrance door. Mark is reading a newspaper while sipping his cup of coffee. I step in, and he looks up, gives me a faint smile and then goes back to his reading.

Hmm, I wonder if I offended him by not calling, I thought.

So to lessen my guilt a little bit, after getting my coffee, I walk up to his table and ask, "Do you mind?" holding lightly the empty chair across him.

"Not at all!" he answers while folding his newspaper and placing it on the side of the table. "So, how've you been?"

Good, at least he talks to me, I thought.

"Busy with work, in fact I've been staying up until the wee hours for the past few nights. On my way here, I felt like a zombie walking up the shop with one strong craving to satisfy…luckily for the people here…coffee appeals to me more," I jokingly say.

Mark quickly counters, "Aw, too bad for me."

Brushing off what he just said, I ask, "What about you? I saw from the card you gave me that you're a lawyer. Are you on a case right now?"

"Oh, I'm a corporate lawyer, not the criminal lawyer that you might think. The only thing that's keeping me busy right now is our pending consolidation with our number one competitor. Well, actually it's exciting in a way that some reporters are calling and hoping to get some scoops about it. Once in a while my name ends up on the paper," he slightly boasts.

"That's nice," I say. I check my watch and it's about time for me to head to work, "Sorry, I have to go. I'll see you around."

"Sure, no problem," he says.

At work, I've been glancing at the time on my computer, and immediately when it turns five in the afternoon, I scramble to pack my stuff and head home.

$$- \varnothing -$$

October 10, 2000 ~ David's Discovery

David called for the second time, and instructed me to do the same thing and left his number to contact him after midnight.

"David! I thought something happened to you last time we talked since I didn't hear from you for a long time. How are you doing?" I asked.

"I'm okay. The guards did random patrolling in the hallway and they thought they heard some noises coming from my quarters. I was able to place the phone back in the Ziploc then hid it in my toilet bowl," he said.

"How did you happen to get a cellphone?" I curiously asked.

"Oh, Ulysses was smart enough to sneak it into the place without getting detected. How? I didn't even bother to ask. He let me use it in times like this," he answered.

This time he was muffling his voice, and started with his updates about the fish tank, "Remember I told you that I would find out what they're hiding in this place?"

"Yes, and ... did you?" I asked.

He then continued, "Well, I did. The underground structure in this island holds three laboratories. I didn't know the last time we talk that there are two more below us. TriXGen went out of their way to recruit top people from different countries to work on a grand plan of surviving in another world. Each recruit is working on individual mastery."

"Did you meet any of them? Or find out what they're up to?" I asked.

"Yes, I did!" he declared.

"A top doctor, they call 'The Prophet', from United Kingdom provides the scientific resource.

"A top engineer, they call 'The Mechanic', from Germany provides the technological resource.

"A top agriculturist, they call 'The Farmer', from Japan provides the agricultural resource.

"The Mechanic is the one I'm reporting to. I frequently assist him when his right-hand man is not available. We are the ones in charge of building the vehicles and artillery needed in some kind of battle. I guess that was how they came up with the name 'The Fort' for this level."

"What about the other ones?" I asked, getting interested in his findings.

David then detailed, "The Farmer created himself an environment that simulates a forest and a farm which they call 'The Greenhouse' on the 2nd lower level.

"And The Prophet is who interests me the most because his lab, called 'The Gallery', occupies the whole 3rd level of the underground structure and has the highest security control.

"I know I can work my way down there. I just need more time."

"You be careful," I told him.

"I will. Anyway, how are Anne and Emily?" he finally asked.

"Oh, Anne still works at the same hospital and is enjoying it. She's currently taking higher education sponsored by the hospital for a chance to move up the ladder and be a Registered Nurse. And Emily just started 5th grade and is looking a lot like her father. By the way, Anne wanted me to tell you how much she misses you. And they will wait for you no matter how long it takes," I relayed.

Whenever the man asked about his family, I felt deep sadness in his voice. I knew David was struggling so hard because he missed them so much, so to ease the guy's pain I offered to send him a picture of his wife and daughter as soon as I could.

~ 0 ~

As I read on in this journal, I'm starting to know what Eric is as a person. And he intrigues me. It sure takes a lot of kindness to go out of his way to help the man and his family.

CHAPTER 14

The Entity in the Coffin

On my scheduled fourth night with the journal, my creative team and I are working diligently to beat the deadline for our upcoming presentation of the final marketing product. Then I have to stay behind after everyone leaves to consolidate the team's completed tasks.

I get home at around 11:45 pm. I'm exhausted and just want to sleep. So, I head straight to my bedroom then drop on my bed, then command, "Lights off!"

The light in my entire place turn off instantly. Aaah…the convenience I get for splurging on a costly installation of a voice automated home automation system that only responds to my voice. The next one I'm eyeing is the keyless entry, and yes, it only responds to my voice so I don't have to worry about a bad guy cutting my finger or hand off just to access my pad.

I turn my body away from the journal. I pull the covers all the way up to cover my chin and snuggle cozily. And suddenly, I hear a thud on the floor behind me.

I sit up and say, "Bedroom lights on!"

To my surprise, the journal is not on the table anymore, but rather on the floor!

Hmm..., I thought.

The spooky feeling takes over my body and it kicks the drowsiness out of me. With all my nerves wide awake, I pick up the journal and decide to read on...

– ∅ –

October 2005 – The Lowest Level

Another five years passed and I knew what to do when I got a call from David.

David figured that no matter how secure any facilities were they need serious clean up. And that was what he worked on.

To get to the lowest level he had to get into the maintenance team. The nice thing about the 'fish tank' was no outside resources were allowed. It was like a country unto itself that didn't allow trading and foreigners. It was an easy task to get acquainted with somebody from the inside of the clean-up crews but how to get in The Gallery was the tricky part. George, one of the survivors from the Blackout Zone, was assigned as one of the cleaners on the level. That was how David got to know about how mysterious The Prophet's lab was. George was the guy who didn't care about anybody's business in the tank, just about his own business cleaning up the lab every Tuesday. After the seclusion, he harbored hatred towards the place and the people running it. He told David that even though they had him and his wife locked up on that place, his loyalty was still to God and his wife that he cared so much about.

David remembered George said something about a cold chamber located at the back of the main lab where only The Prophet had access. Becoming pals with the scientist never crossed his mind so he thought of another easy way to get in.

On George's next scheduled clean-up, he requested to try to do it for him for a day just out of curiosity and see the place that he always talked about. The old man readily handed his id badge to him.

Cleaning was always scheduled at 11:00 pm whether the place was empty or not. That following Tuesday, he did his first risky snooping into the Gallery. Dressed in white hat, white uniform and with cleaning cart, he made his way to the restricted level. As he was about to slide the ID card to open the glass door to the main lab, he spotted the Prophet working late at his lab. The Prophet, seated with his back facing the entrance door, was working diligently with some specs on the microscope, and that gave David a chance to back away. He proceeded to clean up the other rooms down the hall. After an hour, he went back to peek discretely through the glass door to check on the scientist. The room looked clear so he swiped the access card and got into the lab. Just when he thought the Prophet was gone he appeared, walking out of an open hallway leading to the back.

The Prophet upon seeing him said, "You're just in time. I'm done here. Please try not to break anything."

With the white hat covering David's face from head down to his eyebrows, and holding the mop up covering one side of his face, it would be hard for the scientist to recognize him.

While cleaning up, he paid close attention to what was being worked on at the table, he dug in the trash baskets checking out all discarded material for anything that made sense to him before pouring them into his cart. Then he browsed through the things in the storage cabinets while wiping the shelves. And the last thing left to check was the hallway at the back. He made his way to the back while mopping the floor. And there at the end, he found a full metal door without any glass section to see

143

what was inside. The lock was controlled by a security pad located on the wall right beside it. And on top of it was another box that showed the inside temperature of -58 Fahrenheit. It was the lowest possible negative temperature used to preserve a human body for a long period of time. With that, David had accomplished what he came for that day. His next plan was to find out what was behind that metal door. And he knew just how to do it.

David waited a month before he asked his pal again if he could do the clean-up for him. George didn't have a second thought since there wasn't any problem last time he covered for him.

Geared up the same way, he was more confident this time with his ways. He went straight first to the so-called 'cold chamber'. He looked up closely on the security control pad. Then he turned around and walked to a printer located in the corner desk. He opened the printer cover and then removed the cartridges. He reached down into his cleaning cart and grabbed the feather duster. And then, he gently wiped the cartridge holder removing the dust and particles off it. After gathering enough dust on the duster, he walked up to the security control pad and brushed gently on it with the dusty duster. The dust was transferred successfully on four number keys. David then tried punching in different combinations with the four keys and after few minutes the green light lit up followed by a beep. He held on the metal door handle and turned it up counter clockwise. He did it! The door clicked open and he slowly pushed it leaving just a narrow opening, enough to stick his head in to see what was inside.

Behind the door was a small area for putting on the suit hanging on the wall. The suit looked like the space suit that could tolerate the negative temperature in the next room. David put on the suit, then proceeded towards the next metal door. He pushed on a long silver bar located right across the front of the door and it opened inward. After he stepped inside, the door closed automatically behind him.

The room was brightly lit and definitely cold. In the center of the room was a big metallic glass floor freezer. There was a long metal table with wheels pushed against one wall. And on the next wall were two metallic glass cabinets, one contained metal vials with 'X ROE' labels and on the other were metal vials labeled 'Rx Phoenix'. Those things were obvious to David except for the big rectangular container in front of him. What was so special inside that it had to be kept in such an elaborate place? He walked around the metallic freezer and saw a button on one end side of it. Before pressing any button, he decided to check first if the top door would open by just pulling it up by the handle located on the top side of it. So he did . . . and to his surprise it opened. He slowly raised it up until it held itself upright. What he expected to see inside were stocks of frozen rats, frogs or guinea pigs for the Prophet's lab works, but what he saw instead petrified him.

Inside laid a glass coffin with a frozen person in it. David jumped back scared. He paused for a minute to think what to do next. He walked to the end of the tomb where the button was, and pressed it.

The coffin started to rise up and stopped when it reached the top level of the tomb. He examined the body and looked around it to see if there was any information about the person. Unfortunately, he didn't find any. One thing that caught his eye was an elongated dark spot on its left leg about four inches long and two inches wide. There were a few markings on the left arm that looked to be from needle pokes. David couldn't tell by the look of it exactly how long it had been there but it definitely looked fresh. By that time he started to feel cold inside the suit. He hurriedly retracted everything and got out of the chamber.

He cleaned the laboratory as fast as he could and left.

The next day, while working beside the Mechanic, he thought maybe the guy would know something about the Gallery. The man had been around since the startup of the organization. All he needed was to strike up a conversation in the hope that one thing could lead to another. So, he casually asked the man, "Had anybody maneuvered the Capsule already?"

"Well...when I joined the organization, my project leader told me that my job was to fix it and not dig up historical facts about it. Of course, like a little kid I was, I started to dig. What I heard was...it wasn't from here. TriXGen shot it down in New Mexico in 1969 by using an electromagnetic pulse that fried its circuits," he replied.

Then he continued to narrate, "The organization was prepared for its coming.

They transported the Capsule to the bunker in Oakland, Minnesota to hide it. If anybody spotted it in the sky or worse witnessed the crash, they wanted to make sure it won't stay there to be found. In June 1990, I finally completed fixing the wiring and the system went up. But when the bunker caved in, I turned it off. After we shipped it here; we decided not to turn it on until we are sure that it wouldn't be causing any interference with the surroundings, nor to any projects we are working on here including the other divisions. When we finish this first prototype, this will be the first test run. There won't be any surprises since I know the ins and outs of it. Anyway, to answer your question, nobody has flown it yet...except one. There was a pilot on board when it crashed. And as far as I know, that's what the scientist is working on."

After I processed all the information from David, everything started to fall into place.

The Mechanic's Capsule was Thea's Morsel!

— *θ* —

That load of information knocked me to sleep with the journal resting on my chest.

CHAPTER 15

Opens the Pandora's Box

After I finish reading the rest of Eric's journal, there's only one thing for me to do...

I call Mark the next day, Friday. "Hello, Mark? This is Tally. Tally, the zombie, from the coffee shop..." I haven't finished my introduction when Mark acknowledges me.

"Hi, how are you?" he asks. I can hear Mark's excitement, thinking that finally I'm going out with him.

"I'm doing fine. I remember you mentioned that you know someone who works for a newspaper. Is it okay for you to share a name and a contact number with me?" I ask, feeling a little bit guilty about it.

"Oh! I thought you called to...Anyway, sure! Are you ready?" he asks.

"Yes!" I reply.

"Her name is Mary Stiles," he goes on.

After he gives the reporter's phone number to me, I ask, "So, is this coming Monday for a cup of coffee okay with you? Around 1 pm, the usual place?"

There's a pause on his end for a second and then he says, "Yes, that works great!"

"I'll see you then," I say then hang up.

I dial the reporter's number right away. A woman answers, "Hello!"

"Hi, this is Tally McDowell. Can I please speak with Mary Stiles?" I ask.

"This is she. How can I help you?" she asks.

"I have a sensitive high profile story that you may be interested in. It will expose the highest ranking official in the military, who keeps a secret location to carry out his personal agenda," I say in an effort to convince her not to hang up on me.

"Well, I get a lot of that make-believe exposé and in the end they just wanted to get air time on television to be discovered. It's a waste of my time and credibility. How different is your story from theirs?" she asks.

"I'll tell you what's different this time – names, images and the faces of the people involved, all supported by documents. General Adam Bauman is illegally holding innocent victims in this island. The families of these victims have suffered unimaginable pain of not knowing what had happened to them. And even if they learn to accept that they're dead, they're still hurting for not having their bodies to see for the last time," I argue.

It's dead silence on the other line for a few seconds then she says, "I'm free this afternoon. We can meet at Louie's Lounge on the corner of Main and Walton streets. Is 6 pm fine with you?"

"Yes! Meet you at six then," I say.

"By the way, I'll make the reservation under my name," she tells me. "I'll see you then."

We say our goodbyes then we hang up.

I arrive five minutes before six. I give Mary's name at the reservation and a staff person leads me to a corner table for two. When the waiter comes, he asks if I want to order a drink while waiting for Ms. Stiles.

Just to confirm I ask, "I hope you don't mind me asking, how did you know I'm not her?"

The waiter then says, "Oh, Ms. Stiles is a regular here. She meets up with different people a lot of times and always asks for this corner table."

Then I just request a glass of water, no ice, no lemon. My right hand is weighing down on the thick bulging white envelope resting on the right side of the table containing Eric's journal.

My eyes are focused on the entrance door and rarely a lady customer comes alone. So at exactly six o'clock, a petite woman, I guess in her late 30's with dark long wavy hair flowing down over her shoulders, wearing a black blazer over white polo, black pencil cut skirt three inches above her knees and walks with such confidence. She oozes pride in whatever she does. When she reaches the chair across the table, she stops, leans forward, raises her right hand and greets, "Hi! I'm Mary."

I stand up, shake her hand and say, "Tally McDowell. Thank you for meeting me."

We sit down across each other and she starts by saying, "I hope you didn't wait for me to order."

"Oh, I wasn't that hungry," I answer.

"You know, they have good wine here. Do you have any preference?" she asks.

"I pretty much drink any kind. And if it's something I haven't had before then all the better because I like trying new stuff. It looks like you know the place well so I'll just have whatever you're having," I politely answer.

"Alright then," she replies.

The same waiter comes up and greets Mary like she's a generous customer to have in addition to being a regular.

She orders two glasses of 2010 Allegrini wine which is not new to me since I'm a lover of Italian red wine. The wine has the traditional moderate aroma with pleasant fruity taste of raisin with a just-right level of dry sweetness.

Right after the waiter leaves, she starts to ask, "Well, let's see what you have!"

"Before I hand everything to you, you have to give me your word that you're not going to reveal my name no matter what. I don't want to be mobbed. Also, don't ask where I got them. I'm not going to disclose my source as you don't disclose yours," I ask her to promise.

Mary looks at me straight in the eye and says, "I wouldn't be where I am now if I betrayed every person who trusted me. And I don't have any plans of ruining that line of trust. My job is not just work that I have to do to get by and pay my bills. It is my life. And I want my life to have a purpose…a good one if not great. I never intend to hurt innocent people along the way. I may get to the top but those people will hold me down morally and spiritually. Who would enjoy the view from the top when you're alone and sad, and the people you hurt were down below shouting for you to jump. I'm sure Heaven doesn't have an entrance door for that kind of person. I admit that I exposed some people who did unspeakable act of selfishness and wronged others. But I don't think I could ever hurt them anymore because those kinds of people are numb already. I only stop them period."

Mary speaks the entire time without even blinking. "And yes, you have my word," she promises.

Then I proceed by slowly pushing the white envelope towards her and stop in the middle of the table. Without lifting my hand I say, "There's a journal and a cellphone inside this envelope that will give you most of the needed details about the so called TriXGen Corporation."

I pause for a moment when the waiter brings the wine to our table.

And when he leaves, I continue, "Please, call me if you have any questions but after this meeting I prefer not to meet with you in person to avoid any association in the coming events in case you decide to pursue it. I'm really hoping you could publish it and gain the attention required to put an end to it. Maybe crashing the project down to the ground is a long shot but at least freeing the people being held against their will is worth a try.

She's looking me in the eye like she has a truth meter that validates every word I say.

Then she says, "I'll look into it and if I decide to write it then I'll give you a call."

I let go of the envelope. Mary takes it and places it in her handbag. Her bag is sitting on the floor beside her chair on the safe side of the table close to the wall. Then we end our meeting right after finishing our wine.

Weeks pass and I still don't hear anything from Mary. I thought maybe, *the story is too farfetched or too risky for her to pursue*. I can't blame her. General Bauman is the highest military ranking personnel who can command anybody to do a dirty job for him with just a snap of his fingers. And maybe, he could even sink an island in his desperate move to wipe out any evidences against him.

Then after a month, my phone rings. It is a number unknown to me. I let it pass, hoping the caller will leave a message. On the contrary, the caller doesn't leave any message. Then my phone rings again, and it's from the same number. On the third time around, I thought that this call is not a slip of a finger. It could be someone I know and using a different phone, so I decide to answer, "Hello!"

A voice on the other end says, "If you think you can pull it off, you're deluding yourself. You are way over your head. Be careful when you drive. The icy road out there could play a dangerous trick on you."

"Who is this?" I ask in an upset voice.

But I get a dial tone in reply.

My phone rings again and this time my gloves are off, so I answer, "If you think you can scare me with your mafia line well I got bad news for you, my father has a strong tie with a mob boss and…"

"Hello! Tally?! This is Mary. Is it not a good time to speak with you?" she asks at a loss with my greeting.

"Oh, Hi Mary! Pardon me. I thought you were…Anyway, how are you?" I ask.

"Good news. My boss agreed to run the article about General Bauman and his fish tank this coming Sunday on the front page," she announces.

"That's great! Thank you. Thank you so much for making it happen," I say.

"You're welcome. I would have not done it without you. The best details your source provided were the pictures taken from David's cellphone that he forwarded to Eric's cellphone," she says enthusiastically.

"Did everything check?!" I ask amazed in the turn of events.

"Punto per punto!" she replied in her best Spanish accent and added, "The coordinates imprinted on the pictures even pin-pointed the exact location of the island. It took me a while to do the necessary snooping to extract all facts. My boss first was reluctant to do it since it will be a big accusation and scandal. But after having all the documents validated, he finally agreed, but we will be needing help from a higher person than the General just to be safe."

"If you don't mind me asking, who that could be?" I ask, curious who their big gun is.

Without hesitation, she answered, "It turns

out that our newspaper is a big supporter of the newly seated President of the United States. So don't forget to grab a copy. If you have an electronic subscription to The Oakland Journal then you can view it first thing in the morning on Sunday. We will do the push at five in the morning. That's all I called about. And don't worry, nothing will be mentioned about you, Eric or David. The focus will be on General Bauman and his wrong doings. I'll call you if something interesting comes out of it.

"By the way, for my next article maybe you can schedule me for a short meeting with your father. I'm really interested in the life of a mob boss, maybe he can set me up with an introduction."

"Um…Sure! I…I'll ask him," I stutter.

After we hang up the phone, my excitement about the news is overtaken by concern about who the prior caller was and what his intentions are.

With the face identification technology these days, a person can easily be identified, like DNA to a person 30 years ago, but this time it only takes minutes to complete the process. Maybe I was spotted with Mary at that meeting we had more than a month ago. There are a lot of maybes that can drain me mentally, so the way to win over the situation is to face it head on. *Bring it on* is my new morning mantra now. I guess my *Today is the day* motto will have to take the backseat until this entire issue passes.

Sunday morning comes and I decide to take a walk around the block. On my way back home I pass by my favorite breakfast diner, so I decide to pop in for a coffee and check the morning paper. I also plan to enjoy their famous Fontina cheese croissant that makes my mouth water even just thinking about it.

Unfortunately, the newspaper stand by the receiving area is empty. I thought for a moment that they didn't put out any newspapers at all. But when I glance inside the dining area, most customers where holding newspapers and busy reading them. And I happen to zero in on one, and there at the front page of The Oakland Journal is a headline that reads, 'General Adam Bauman in a Conspiracy Beyond the Call of Duty!'

I decide to head back home instead, and grab my own copy of the newspaper at a convenience store beside my apartment building.

The article doesn't disclose the name and location of the island to prevent people from charging to the place. But everything about the place and the activities taking place are meticulously detailed. And General Bauman was accused of abuse of power, illegal detention, and conspiracy just for starters. And it is mentioned that his two main goals were first, for humans to achieve life sustainability and longevity in another world; and second, and more important to him, was to achieve a five-star rank when war broke out between the two worlds.

The article finishes with the statements, "In the end, there is no fear of invasion here on earth after all, but humans invading the world out there. If we succeed, then what's next?"

After the article was published I receive a bouquet of flowers from Eric with a note thanking me for taking the risk.

CHAPTER 16

Treasure at the End of the Rainbow

The news attracts nationwide media attention. This results in groups of different factions across the nation staging protests asking the government to expose the truth.

The uproar is national but the attention goes global. The newly elected president of the United States, President Mercer, now in first few months of his term, promises the people that he will bring the walls of secrecy down and let the truth out.

He starts by demanding the immediate arrest of General Bauman.

In his press appearance, he mentions that he doesn't believe there's any reason why any of such undertakings must be kept secret. For those who believe, then it is not a problem; for those who don't, then they can just ignore it; and for those who don't care, then let's move on.

TriXGen is dissolved and a private company with the highest bid is chosen to take over the project. The president forms a committee that will work with the company to oversee its dealings, since the Capsule and everything associated with it are still the country's prized possessions.

The Prophet takes his turn to bask in the spotlight when he opens to the public the chance to participate in his program called 'RxPhoenix' that will test the serum he developed to fight aging and cancer. There will be draws every year for three potential candidates for the program. Each candidate has the option to accept it; reject it, then another draw will be made; or pass it to someone else that he or she chooses. Whichever way it goes, three persons every year will have the chance to live longer.

Everyone who was detained in the island is given the choice to stay or go back home.

Ulyses and San marry and leave for Thailand. San is now pregnant with their first child.

George lost his wife in the island. She died from natural causes. The one thing that he fought for was for his wife to stay the way she was, in her truest form as human. Not to get altered. He can't wait to see his grandchildren and great-great-grandchildren when he leaves the place.

Friday, March 1, 2030; Eric picks up Anne, who's now on her 60's, and Emily, now 38 years old, and invited them to celebrate his birthday and spend the weekend at his place.

"So Uncle Eric, how old are you now?" Emily asks Eric.

"Didn't your Mom teach you that it's not polite to ask a person's age?" he answers.

"Well, you're family to us. And we're supposed to be more forgiving. Also, I lost track of your age since nothing changed in you since I remember first knowing you. So, back to my question," she persists, true to her vigorous nature.

"I'm 78," he awkwardly answers, knowing the obvious mismatch with his present look.

When they get to his place, as he drives up slowly to the front of his house, a man opens the front door and walks out to meet them.

Anne sees the man who's walking towards the car as it slows down to park. She intently stares at him and her eyes start to get watery. She reaches for her daughter's hand, kisses it and starts to cry.

"Mom, are you okay? What's wrong?" Emily asks.

"Nothing's wrong my dear. Everything is good now," she replies.

The moment the car stops, the man opens the passenger door on Thea's side. She gets off the car and jumps right into the man's arms.

Emily immediately hops out of the car to see what's happening. And when she gets the glimpse of the man her mother is hugging so tight, she mutters, "Dad?!"

David and Anne hug each other for a long time. It is a scene so familiar to Eric 41 years ago and tears start to rundown on his face.

Emily walks around the car to meet with her father. When David sees her coming, he walks up to her, hugs her, and lifts her off the ground like she's still daddy's little girl.

When Anne joins them, David says to her, "I told you I would see you and Emily again." Then they all hug together and cry. During his absence, Anne never stopped talking about him to their daughter and showing his pictures to her. That's the reason why Emily grew up knowing her father and understanding why he got separated from them.

David receives financial compensation from the government, enough for him and his family to live comfortably and be able to start building happy memories as a whole family that was once deprived of them for decades. And yet, he still decides to keep his job on the island under the new management. The challenges and knowledge he gets from building advance technological vehicles can never be equaled someplace else.

The government is now building a museum named 'The Gallery' at the site where it crashed, and will house the actual Morsel. And it will be open for public viewing.

Thea is glad to know that she will soon get the chance to see the Morsel without any obstacles or hurdles. And the most important of all is she knows where to find it when it's time for them to leave.

Right after I met with Eric, the ghost train stopped showing up as he predicted.

Days pass and everything in my life starts to get back to normal. Then I receive a call from my mother telling me that they received a check with a note telling them that the previous owner of the land wanted to extend his apology by reimbursing them the money that they lost due to the past life history of the property that they unintentionally forgot to disclose. What's odd to them is that the sender finished the note with the word "END", which they had only seen on telegrams in their early years.

Summer draft is in the air, trees are standing proud with their leaves green and full, flowers have bloomed and are looking straight up at the sun. And her I am at a stand-still, missing some actions that Eric had brought in my life the past months.

June 2030, as I'm sluggishly cleaning up my place on a weekend, my phone rings. It's Eric!

"Remember the second issue you had about me when we first met? I'm trying to work on it and I'm hoping maybe you could join me for a dinner next Saturday, your choice of restaurant? This time I'll pick you up," he invites.

With coyness on my part, I answer, "Um, I need to check my schedule and will let you know."

We chat for a while about little happenings in our days. After we hang up, I feel like I get thrown back in time during my college days when the popular varsity player invited me to go out. I was so ecstatic and felt validated that amongst my group of girlfriends he chose me.

I proceed to clean my bathroom. And as I'm looking at the mirror, I notice a bright aura and a smile in my face that I'd lost for a long time. It really feels good to have it back. I know now that this is the start of a new life for me next to immortality.

CHAPTER 17

Who is General Bauman?

The General is found guilty after the 30 days of speedy trial in a court-martial. He is sentenced immediately at the time of the verdict to seven years and could be out in three for good behavior.

Locked in his cell, the General is writing on a piece of paper. After he finishes writing, he places it in a short brown envelope, seals it then writes the name of the recipient in the center. He puts it in his inmate-shirt chest pocket. Then he takes a cotton ball out of a small carton box a size of jewelry box and picks up his plastic cup half full of water. He sits on his bed and places the cotton ball and the water cup on the floor. He folds up his left leg pant. Then, he carefully scrapes a piece of skin on the outer side of his left leg below the knee. When he finishes peeling the thin soft rubbery skin-liked material off his leg, an elongated dark spot about four inches long and two inches wide shows on his skin. He is covering it to hide that one piece of evidence that reveals his true identity. That marking is something that his kind can never alter. It identifies one from the others. When Usil was captured inside the Morsel by TriXGen, he was unconscious, but still alive.

– 0 –

1969 New Mexico

The Morsel crashed in the middle of two mountains outside the populated area in Albuquerque, New Mexico. A beacon discovered as early as 1920 was the catalyst that made the TriXGen Corporation prepared for the next arrival of another sort. And that effort paid off on the day of the capture of the occupant and the possession of the Morsel.

The occupant was assigned to the British scientist who immediately performed all necessary tests to make sure it didn't possess any threat to human health. He then labeled the occupant 'X Roe'.

After a few days of testing and placing X Roe under sedation, General Bauman, a four-star general in the U.S. Army who led the group, decided to see what the occupant from another world looked like.

Alone and contained in a secured room, X Roe suddenly opened his eyes. His head, wrists and ankles were strapped down at the examination table. He could feel that he was covered with a sheet from waist down. He rolled his eyes from side to side to check his surroundings. The room was pretty much bare. Then he heard the door being opened. He closed his eyes to pretend to stay unconscious.

The Brit scientist came in followed by General Bauman and his right-hand military man, Sgt. Clyde Lunden. They stopped and stood a few yards away from the table where X Roe was lying and very much aware of what was happening in the room. He was relaxing his whole body and not reacting to any disturbances. He was waiting for the right time to get out of the situation in a well-planned manner.

"It looks so much like us," the General said to the scientist.

"I put it under sedation right now until I complete thorough tests on it. If you will excuse me, I'll get the copy of its X-Ray for you to see," the scientist said then left the room.

The General cautiously started to take steps closer to the table only stopping an inch short to the side of it. Standing tall at six feet and two inches on the right side of X Roe, he slowly moved his head from left to right staring down at the uncanny similarities to a human. Then he lifted his right hand off his side over to X Roe's body and gently placed the tip of his index finger on its mid chest to have a sense of how it feels to the touch. Instantly, a strong electrical charge ran from X Roe's chest and flowed through the General's finger. The General started to jolt. Sgt. Lunden then grabbed onto the General's shoulders in an attempt to pull him away but he too started to get electrocuted. Then after a few seconds they both dropped down to the floor unconscious.

X Roe's body generated enough heat that all the straps that held him down burned and broke.

He immediately got off the table and then knelt down on both knees beside the General. He placed his hands on the sides of the General's head. Then electrical charge started to flow with bright lights running in a cycle that went from one body to another. Their faces and bodies started to change features. By the time the current stopped flowing, each man looked like the other. They had switched appearances!

X Roe then took the General's clothes off and put them on himself. He picked up the General's body and placed it on the table. Then he left a burn mark on the General's left leg similar to his.

X Roe then went down to Sgt. Lunden and placed his palms on Sgt. Lunden's chest. At that instant, Sgt. Lunden started to come out of it. He helped him stand up and told him that he was able to stop the occupant from escaping while he was out from getting shocked. The scientist walked in and noticed the disarray on the table and the sergeant was still dazed and weak and being held up by the General, so he asked, "What happened?"

"He woke up and tried to escape but I was able to overcome him. I think I knocked him out. You have to use better restraints than these," X Roe, who now owned the General's identity, said.

~ 𝜌 ~

After the General finishes cleaning the ID mark on his left leg, he puts back the fake skin that covers it and he's now ready to receive his visitor.

His first weekend of scheduled visitation for inmates arrives. He, together with the other inmates who have visitors, is taken to the guest receiving room. Waiting at one table is Sgt. Lunden. The General walks up to him and while they shake hands, the General says, "I appreciate you coming here. A nine-hour drive wasn't an easy task, my friend."

"No problem. How are you doing," the Sergeant asks.

"I'm doing fine. The barracks are pretty calm. I still get to enjoy a lot of personal services, food cart and TV. The only different now is the tight space. Other than that there's no better place for me to spend a decade of confinement," he replies with a hint of satisfaction with the outcome of his conviction.

"How's your wife doing now?"

"She's doing a lot better now. She gained back the weight she lost and turned into an organic nut," the visitor replies with a tone of gratitude.

When the visiting time is over, the two men stand up and firmly shake hands. The General's other hand takes the brown envelope out of his pocket and attempts to pass it discreetly to the sergeant and says, "Please make sure the Mechanic gets it."

"But...I thought you are prevented from having any contacts with anybody in the new organization?" suspicious about the General's action, the sergeant questions and hesitant to touch the envelope.

"Yes, but you're not aware of that, right?" he places his right hand on the visitor's left shoulder and gives a little squeeze making sure his friend gets the point.

So the Sergeant, without saying a word, takes it then pushes it in his front pocket folding it in the process.

"You take care, my friend," says the General.

Then they part ways.

CHAPTER 18

Returning a Favor

On our first date, my first question to him is, "How on earth did you pull off the act of creating the terror at the diner?"

"I crept in the dark of the night on the sides and under the front window of your parents' diner when no one was around. Then I placed my devices that beamed the image and produced realistic rumbling sounds of a runaway train. Have you heard of the new SIM technology?" he pauses for a few seconds for my answer.

All he gets from me is a blank stare, so he continues, "Anyway, I placed one portable projector in front of the diner that created and projected a simulation of a moving train with its surroundings in a 3D effect. Then my two components on the sides of the diner at the same time produced the associated sounds, vibrations and sensations within the set ranges in the apparatus. Just imagine if you were in the middle of them, which I think you experienced, it will be a blast," he says excitedly with a sense of pride and accomplishment.

But all I'm hearing is blah, blah, blah...and say, "That wasn't cool for my parents, though."

In this era of 3Ds and holograms, even my own 3D reflection in the mirror brushing my teeth still spooks me...I should have known better.

"I'm really sorry about that. I was as desperate for help as you were desperate for clues," he says with remorse.

"In case you're interested to know, my parents used the money they received from the previous owner of their land to give away discount coupons, free meals, and free samples at the door. Later on, the diner flourished and my parents couldn't be happier," I add.

"Oh, I'm happy to hear that!" he says.

Then our waiter comes up with two glasses of red wine. Eric seems to be expecting it since he nods at the waiter and the waiter nods back at him. The waiter sets them on our table, one for each of us, then walks away.

Eric picks up his glass of wine and gestures for a toast and says, "Here's to the start of an extraordinary friendship!"

For a while I thought of saying, *here's to long life* but it may be an understatement or plain sad truth to him so instead I toast, "to life's endless possibilities!"

I feel so contented for the first time in my life having him sitting across me and laughing with him. I haven't experienced such company for a long time since I broke up with my first boyfriend 16 years ago. His eyes speak to me more than words can say. His smile shows me how happy he is to spend every second that passes. And his voice lingers in my ears like a sweet melody.

The bubbles in my head pop when the waiter comes up and asks if we care for another glass. But I make it my rule to just have one glass whenever it's a meeting outside my group of friends. I need to maintain my inhibitions so not to ruin the first impression.

Eric and I go out every now and then, and just spend time discussing about the sensational exposé.

Summer is ending and I'm enjoying one lazy

Sunday afternoon in my couch when flash news cuts off my regular programming to make way for a latest update that happened late last night. A familiar face happens to be on the news flash alert.

"Mary Stiles, a well-known correspondent for the Oakland Journal, is in critical condition at the Angel of Mercy Hospital right now after her car went out of control and fell off the overpass south of highway M59 last night. No further details have been released about what caused the accident. As of this moment, the investigation is still on-going," the newscaster reports in a very serious manner that reflects deep sympathy to one of his colleagues in the business.

Then, my phone rings and it's Eric. "We need to pay her a visit at the hospital," he states, neither asking for my consent nor if I know about the accident.

"If you're talking about Mary then I don't even know if we will be allowed to see her at this point because of her delicate state. Doctors might only allow immediate family members. It will be a long shot," I say.

"I hear your concern but we need to try. I doubt that it was an accident, and if we need to become immediate family members to get in then that's what we are going to be. We will go in after the visiting hours around ten in the evening when it's less crowded with staff and visitors. Down time tends to vacuum the staff's energy to argue," he persists.

Eric calls me up when he drives up in front of my apartment building. I run outside and hop in Eric's car. "Tally, meet Thea and Zian," introducing me while looking back over his shoulder.

I look back and smile at them and say, "Nice to meet you!"

"Nice to formally meet you too, regardless of the current situation we're in," Thea greets back.

"Hi!" Zian greets with a timid smile.

Then I turn to face Eric and ask, "So what's your plan?"

"You think you can find a way to put on a hospital uniform?" he asks with hesitation. "That will give as an advantage to move around with a little ease."

"Um...Yeah sure! Let me check my bag for one. Oops! Sorry I left my bag at my place. You know I'm a creative marketing lead by profession. It's not in my credentials to pose as someone I'm not. How in the world will I do that?" I ask with a bit panic in my voice.

"We'll figure it out when we get there," he calmly replies.

When we enter the hospital lobby, I ask them to wait. I walk around looking for a male doctor and that's when I spot one with the name embroidered on the gown, Dr. Love, Endocrinologist, relaxing at the cafeteria. He's more into his health magazine than a bowl of salad still untouched on the table in front of him. That's all the information I need to move to my next step.

I walk to the information desk and ask the staff, "Hi! I'm Dr. Love's new secretary and it's my first day at work so I'm not that familiar with the area. He accidentally spilt his drink all over himself and asked me in a hurry to get him a new gown to change. I'm trying to impress him, but honestly I don't know where to get it. Can you please help me?"

The staff person picks up the phone and dials a number while smiling sheepishly and then speaks, "Hi, Julie. This is Susan upstairs. Dr. Love is requesting the usual and as always a new secretary..." she pauses and asks me, "What's your name?"

"Nadia," I answer.

"Her name is Nadia and she's coming down there to pick it up," she ends the conversation with a few more remarks and laughter like she knows Dr. Love with a reputation that is worthy to poke fun at.

After she directs me where the stairs down to the staff cleaning service room, I thank her then go my way.

Eric is standing by the post, waiting vigilantly while the mother and son are seated comfortably in the sofa of the lobby watching TV.

I go straight to Eric then grab him by the wrist with my right hand while I'm concealing the rolled up dry cleaned doctor's gown under my left arm.

I pull him in a hurry forgetting for a moment that he's walking with a cane, then we stop in front of the men's restroom. I press the gown on his chest and demand, "Here, put this on. It's your turn to be on front lines."

His left hand instinctively holds on to it, since his right hand is dedicated to his cane. Confused with what I just said, he says, "But..."

I immediately cut what he is about to say in his eerily shocked state and say, "No buts. Hurry up and change. I'll wait out here."

When he comes out, I almost burst into laughter. The gown, meant for a smaller physique than his, looks to be choking every vein in his arms and upper body.

"You didn't look hard enough for someone my size," he says in dismay while struggling to pull the sleeves to cover more the length of his arms.

"It's not as bad as you think," I counter, trying to cover up that one oversight in my plan.

"I don't have to think. I can feel it," he sarcastically says in a soft voice close to my right ear. "I knew you were a natural. Now, what's next?"

"We're going to the emergency receiving desk. And you will tell them that you are trying to help us find Mary, my sister. I don't think Dr. Love is a familiar face in an emergency unit so you will be fine."

Thea and Zian are stunned to see him in a gown. They try to hold their laughter, showing only slight grins in their faces.

Eric leads the way to the North Wing of the hospital where the ER is located. When he reaches the receiving desk, he speaks to the female staff behind the desk, "Hi, I have a woman who got lost in our wing looking for Mary Stiles, her sister. She saw on the news this morning that Ms. Stiles was taken here last night. Could you please look her up and let her know which room her sister is in."

The staff looks something up on the computer then says, "I'm sorry doctor..." the woman pauses checking the name tag on Eric's white coat, then proceeds on saying, "Love, but she is in critical condition and no visitor is allowed at the moment, not even immediate relatives."

Zian, who is just behind Eric standing at the end of the counter by the entryway, sees the need to help out in a dead-end situation they're in. A gush of strong wind passes in the area and the papers and other light stuff sitting on the desk are blown away up in the air, including the woman's open bag of chips. The woman gets off her chair and panics to gather the papers on the floor and at the same time saying, "Where in the world did that wind come from?"

The boy steps in and helps the woman pick up the mess on the floor. Eric takes the chance to look on the computer monitor and check which room Mary is in.

"Thank you anyway. Have a nice day!" he quickly bids goodbye to the inattentive staff busy sorting the papers.

Then we all sneak in through the wide door pass the receiving desk.

"Rooms 101 – 105, to the right," Eric directs us at the end of the hall.

"Here it is, room 103."

He gently opens the door and peeks in the room. Suddenly, a voice inside speaks to him, "Hi! Are you going to check on her?"

Eric composes himself, then steps inside the room leaving us in awe outside not knowing what to do next.

Then the door opens and a man in his 70's walks out, shakes our hands while saying, "The doctor said you're close friends of my daughter. Thank you for coming. You can go in now, the doctor said it's okay."

We step inside while I'm literally lost. What in the world we are doing there rushing in like that in the first place. *Why can't we wait and pay a visit in a traditional relaxed way…with flowers?* I ask myself. *Why sneak in, in the dead of night without anybody around as if we are up to no good?*

Mary is lying in the bed; her head is wrapped in bandage. I can't recognize her face from the last time I saw her. Somehow it is a bit reassuring to see her less wired than what I imagine somebody in a critical condition. With only the oxygen and heart monitor attached to her, she looks more relaxed. The scene is understating the trauma she is experiencing deep inside.

"Her father told me that the previous doctor who checked on her said that she is in coma due to the impact that she suffered from the accident. I thought we can talk to her and ask what really happened. If somebody did this to her because of the help she gave us, then that person needs to pay. I can't just turn my back on her. I must help her," Eric says out loud.

"Eric, let me try. Zian is here to help if something goes wrong," Thea offers in sympathy while holding her son's hand tight to her side. "The only way to find out if everything goes right is for her father to ask her one important event in her life that only they know."

I'm getting lost in the conversation so I just stand in one corner and let them do what they have to do.

Eric steps back too, to make way for Thea to step forward. She stays on the clear side of the bed, opposite the side where the tube and wire run between Mary and the machines. She places her right hand on Mary's head while her left hand is holding Mary's wrist like she's checking her pulse. Zian is standing by the foot of the bed and Eric stands with his back against the door as if to block anyone who tries to come in.

Then as I'm standing puzzled with what Thea is doing I notice that her right hand resting on Mary's head starts to illuminate. In a matter of seconds it brightly lights up and fills the entire room. It makes it hard for me to keep my eyes open to see what is taking place at that time so I try to block the bright light by placing my hands in front of my eyes but as fast as it comes it goes, too.

Thea steps back. In less than a minute, Mary starts to open her eyes and slowly moves her head to check her surroundings. That's the signal for Eric to go outside and get her father. When they come back in, the father knows what to do already. He walks toward his daughter, bends down and whispers something to her. Then he puts his left ear close to her lips and she says something back to him. The father then starts to cry then hugs his daughter like everything is fine now.

Mr. Stiles wipes the tears from his face then turns to Eric and utters, "Thank you!"

"Mr. Stiles, if you don't mind, I need to ask your daughter a few questions about the accident," Eric says.

"Not at all," the father says, and then faces his daughter, "I'll be outside."

Eric steps closer to Mary then asks, "Hello Mary! Do you remember what happened the night of the accident?"

Mary nods once then gulps before uttering the word, "Yes."

Then she continues in a very mild voice, "When I got into my car, a man appeared right behind me in the backseat. He was pointing a knife to my side and commanded me to drive around. He wanted to know where I got all the information about General Bauman and the island. When I didn't tell him anything, he directed me to the direction of the flyover. Before I reached the curve at the top, he jumped out. Then after a few seconds something blew up underneath the car and it went out of control."

She stops for a few seconds to remember what she can, then adds, "I also remember that before the bridge incident, he said sorry to me for what was about to happen. He said that he was only returning a favor. He said that the General he knew before had the integrity and honor of a decent man. But everything changed in him after the capture of the pilot from the Capsule. He even started to behave distant from the people who cared about him. He was cold if not insensitive towards them. He even wondered when he caught the General hiding a dark elongated spot on his left leg that maybe the General had some kind of infection in his body that was causing him to behave indifferently."

Thea then jumps in the conversation and asks, "Are you sure about the man mentioning the dark elongated spot on the left leg of the General?"

"Yes. After the man mentioned it, I asked myself, *why anyone would hide something as petty as that?*" she replies.

"You will be fine now," Eric assures Mary. "We'll let you rest."

I can't leave without showing myself to her, so I step forward, touch Mary's left hand and say, "Hey, I'm so sorry for what happened. Get some rest and I'll talk to you later."

She manages to give me a relaxed smile now, and that's when I notice that the bruises on her face start to fade.

Now, another challenge is how to pass by the receiving desk without the staff noticing us and call the security. When we come out of the door, another gush of wind swirl in her station again and she ends up right where we left her...catching the papers blown up in the air. So it is an easy get away for us.

Eric drives Thea and Zian home first. After they get off the car, I confront Eric, "Now tell me what just happened at the hospital. I think I deserve an explanation."

The car starts to slow down, then he parks on the side of the road. He starts saying, "Thea and Zian are special beings. They are not from here."

"What do you mean? Out of state? Country? What made them special then?" I ask.

"It turned out that there are other worlds out there. Based on what I gathered from Thea, there are three, The Gaulkan which is the holy; The Ganti which is the impious; and our world which is the uncertain. They are immortals from Gaulkan with unique abilities. Thea believe that somehow the entity from Ganti got into their world and brought darkness to their leader. It had never happened before that the unholy crossed to their world. Right now it is chaotic in Gaulkan. They're here to get refuge and will go back when it's safe," Eric explains while studying my reactions.

After Eric finishes, I feel like I just woke up this morning in a totally unknown time and space. I don't even know how to react anymore, and my mind is having a hard time processing everything he just said. When he can't get any response out of me he starts to drive.

"I can get off here," telling him to stop the car at the corner of my block.

Before I hop out of the car, he holds on to my left arm to stop me for a moment and says, "I'm sorry to put you through all these. I won't blame you if you don't want to see me again. Please don't base your judgment about me on the oddity of the situation I'm in. I didn't ask for this. Still I tried to get things resolved the best way I can rather than be bitter about it. I may live hundreds of years here on earth, so I want to make sure it's not going to be miserable one."

After he said that, I proceed to get out of the car. I don't hear the car driving away behind me, so either he is waiting for me to look back or making sure I'll get in safe. I walk towards my apartment building, go in and never look back.

After a week, Sgt. Lunden is captured as an accessory to the crime masterminded by Gen. Bauman. Mary was able to identify him from the line of visitors with constant meeting with the General inside the barracks. And in the end the General is put to a maximum security they called 'The Box'; and his phone and visitation privileges are taken away.

CHAPTER 19

Out of Sight

Eric is 30,000 feet up in the sky on a flight to South Korea. He just accepted a contract-job for three weeks to check the architectural design plan of the upcoming high-rise commercial building that will be situated in the heart of Seoul City.

It seems to take forever, sitting and waiting for his plane to reach its destination with his head full of the jumble of events that happened over the past few weeks. And most of all, he can't seem to get Tally out of his mind. He's sad that they parted on a sour note which was the last thing he wanted to do to a person he holds dear to his heart. But then he's taking this assignment as a good break for everyone to have some time to think and breathe a fresh air of perspective. And helps him gets his mind off Tally.

Dying his hair grey gives a nice touch of salt and pepper color on it, and a few fine lines on the forehead to match his age and picture on his passport; and he passes the immigration check without a question. When he exits the terminal gate he spots a lady holding a sign with his name on it. He walks up to her and says, "Hi, I'm Eric Dutton!"

The woman smiles, raises her hand for a handshake and says, "Joh-eun ahchim-ipnida!"

Not knowing how to react or answer to what she said, Eric shakes her hand and immediately informs her, "I'm sorry but I can't speak Korean."

"Pardon me. I'm Shin Pae. Please, this way," she says, then gestures in the direction of the terminal parking lot exit.

"I will be your guide during your stay here."

"That's great!" he says.

Shin Pae is taller than average Korean woman with medium straight black hair, Asian dramatic eyes, pink thin lips, and she has a wide sweet smile that can magically wake up any man's sleeping heart. But the way she dresses contradicts all that. She wears a blue long-sleeve polo tucked neatly into black slacks and walks with ease on black high heel shoes. If she didn't introduce herself as his guide she would have been mistaken as a detective.

"Mr. Dutton, are you hungry? Do you want to stop to eat before I drop you off at your hotel?" she asks with mild Asian accent.

"Oh, I'm fine. I just want to head straight to my hotel and get some rest," he answers. "But thanks for the offer."

During the ride, Eric takes the luxury to enjoy the site of harmonious blend of century old and modern architectural buildings in the bustling metropolis. Then Shin points to her right out in the distance where a vacant piece of land is situated and says, "That's where the new building will be standing."

Then after five minutes they reach the hotel right at the bottom end of downtown area away from the busy streets but with a great view of the Seoul's skyline.

Before Eric hops out of the car, Shin hands him her personal card and says, "Please give me a call if you need anything. I'll pick you up at the lobby tomorrow morning at eight to take you to meet Mr. Lang."

Eric takes the card and says, "Thank you. I'll see you tomorrow."

When he checks the card, the title under Shin's name says, "Personal Security, Tour Guide and Private Investigator."

The next day, Eric can't help and ask Shin during the ride, "So what do you really do?"

"I knew I should've ordered new cards," Shin says while grinning then continues, "Every person I hand it to seems to get confused. I'm a private investigator. I resigned as a cop a year ago, and tour guide is my side line.

"Mr. Lang, your recruiter, is my regular client. He frequently asks me to accompany his guys, especially those from outside of the country, to visit places that might require an experienced security person to keep them away from trouble. I know the rules and I'm making sure that they are following them. So far, I haven't failed him yet."

"Well, I don't think I'll be going around that much. I'll do my job as fast as I can then leave," he says.

Shin doesn't respond, as if ignoring his brush off.

When they get to the building where Mr. Lang has an office, Shin parks at the fourth level then instructs Eric, "There's a door straight ahead to access the floor and Mr. Lang's office is 401. I'll wait here."

Then after an hour, Eric comes out holding a few rolls of drawings. "Please take me to the site so I can conduct some surveys in the area. It might just take 30 minutes then I'll work the rest of the day at my hotel room," he says to Shin.

That night after working hard, Eric decides to take a walk downtown to check the city by night. And it's the most awake city he's ever been to. It's ten at night and the streets are still bustling with people and all establishments are well lit up with flashing lights to win some patrons.

He decides to go in this one bar that looks the tamest, and the subdued lighting is indicative of quiet ambiance inside, perfect for unwinding, he assumes.

Indeed the place is empty and Eric sits at the bar. He relaxes over a glass of beer while staring at the TV showing a local news which he can't understand, except the pictures and videos being shown.

"Where you from?" the bartender asks in a very strong Korean accent which Eric doesn't get first.

"I'm sorry?" he responds.

"You..." the bartender pointing at him then asks, "what country from?"

"Oh, from America," he replies.

"Nice!" the man counters.

Then a woman enters and sits at the end of the bar. The bartender takes her order and starts to work on it. Eric goes to the restroom and when he comes back he sees the woman sitting at the end crying, "Aniyo!"

A few basic Korean words Eric can understand and that is one of them. She kept repeating that same word meaning 'no' to a man who's sitting beside her and looks like giving her distress.

Shin's words keep echoing in his head, *stay away from trouble*. The Caucasian man, twice the size of the petite Korean woman, grabs her by the arm to the point of making her scream in pain. At this point, Eric can't just sit and be deaf about it so he walks up to them and asks, "Is everything ok?"

The man turn his head to check him and says, "Who the heck are you?"

"I just…" Eric doesn't finish what he's going to say when strong hands from behind grab him by the shoulders. He's dragged to the door and thrown outside. He lands on his butt, and when he sees the man standing at the door, he's a size of a sumo! Eric is ready to get up and take his chance to tackle the guy when out of nowhere Shin blocks him from taking another step forward and says, "I think you had enough."

Eric calms down and walks away with Shin not because he's afraid but rather worried that Shin will be caught in the middle.

"Were you following me?" Eric suspiciously asks.

"Yes, and I get paid for it," she replies. "I told you to call me if you need to get around town."

"I didn't do anything wrong," he says in a serious tone. "I can take care of myself."

"I see, that was why your butt was kissing the ground there for a second," she sarcastically counters.

"You should have waited. I could have deflated that guy," Eric still trying to convince Shin to give him some chance to prove himself.

"There's a lot more where that big guy came from. They're called *waegukin clan*. A non-Korean gang that has been doing some crimes in the area and seems to get away with them. I worked on one of its cases and the individual that we caught didn't break his silence. They call it retirement once they're caught. It seems like the family of any such individual will be well taken care of. I kept pursuing it until they kidnapped my daughter. They returned her unscathed. It was my decision to resign to protect her," Shin reveals with a deep sad look in her face.

Now Eric stands down and feels sorry for her. He then asks, "You didn't mention you have a kid."

"Well, you didn't ask." she replies.

"It wasn't appropriate then, so where's the father of your child?" he asks.

"My husband is in the army right now," she answers as they approach the front of Eric's hotel. "You better get some rest. I'll see you tomorrow."

The entire night, Eric's mind is occupied with information from Shin. *Stay away from that place. That bar is like a front where the group hangs and discusses their illegal dealings*, Shin had warned him.

After less than three weeks, Eric finishes his work and scheduled to fly back in two days. The day before he leaves, he visits the bar again. It is a chilly night and raining. As he expects, based on the reputation of the bar, he's the only customer that night.

He sits at the same chair and it is the same guy attending at the bar. What Eric is not aware of is that behind the kitchen door are cameras that monitor the inside and outside premises of the bar but don't record. The man who sees him on the monitor recognizes him from the last incident. He goes to the back door that leads to another secret room where Mr. Monti, the leader of the group and the same man Eric approached last time at that bar, is working on some computation on the book.

"Mr. Monti, the same American from a couple of weeks ago is in the house," the man informs.

"I got it," he says then picks up the phone and dials a number. "Hey, Joe get the gang here right now."

After a couple of minutes, the front door swings open and a gang of heavyweight men appears. The same sumo looking guy walks straight to him, grabs his drink then pour out the contents onto the floor and says, "You think you're tough?"

Eric ignores him and orders another glass from the bartender. Two men scoop him by the arms and take him in the middle of the room, pushing clear some tables to make more space. Then Mr. Monti comes out from the back and sounding his knuckles. He gives Eric a low hard punch in the stomach without any word. He is about to do it again when Eric uses the two men holding him to swing his legs up landing a kick on Mr. Monti's chin. He then pulls his body down to the floor with full force to free him from the men's restraints. Mr. Monti's men start jumping on him but they are quickly repelled by lines of electric current coming from Eric's body. All the men are thrown back and Mr. Monti is at the corner, frozen in shock by what he is witnessing. Eric for the first time experiences the phenomenal ability caused by the accident decades ago in the Blackout Zone. He takes that advantage to walk up to Mr. Monti and strikes him with a small amount of electricity just to warn him and says, "I'll be watching you. And when you or any of your men make one false move, I'll be there to fry you."

Eric calms himself down and the electric current that runs in his entire body suddenly turns off. Nobody dares to jump him at that point so he just walks out of the place leaving everyone shocked including himself.

The next day, Shin picks him up to take him to the airport. Upon driving by Mr. Monti's bar, she notices the sign at the door that says *Temporarily closed for business*.

"That's a first," Shin utters.

"What?" Eric asks.

"That bar never closes, not even on holidays!" Shin answers.

"By the way, thank you for your time to drive me around and most of all for protecting me. You should go back to what you really love doing, and ... I don't think Mr. Monti will cause you any more troubles," Eric tells Shin, trying to give her some encouragement to pursue her love of being a cop.

Before Shin could ask Eric how he knew about Mr. Monti, Eric's cellphone rings. He reach for it from his hand carry then answers, "Zian! How are you?"

They talk for a while until they reach the airport. "Zian, I need to go. I'll see you at dinner time," Eric hangs up then hops out of the car to grab his luggage at the backseat.

Shin gets off the car and stands right by the driver seat and says, "By the way, how did you know about Mr. Monti?"

"Oh, just heard about him. Anyway, I'm running late! Thanks for everything!" Eric walks away from the car without giving Shin the chance to force more details out of him.

On his flight back home, Eric already concocts a plan to warn the Prophet about his vaccine before his program starts without giving away his identity. It's important that the scientist test it thoroughly in animals placed in a hostile environment. The presence of predators could aggravate or provoke the subject to react, thus changing the reaction to the vaccine.

For his personal realizations, he now has the hard task of controlling his emotion and allowing his anger to overtake him. And the most awakening of all is that the absence from home didn't help a bit to forget Tally. The distance only made his heart miss her more. But he is not ready yet. For he knows the sad truth that no matter what the nature of the circumstances might be, he will be left alone in the end to endure the pain of losing someone he loves. And just thinking about the inevitable hurts him already.

CHAPTER 20

Déjà vu

I haven't heard anything from Eric since that peculiar happenings on the day that we visited Mary. Maybe I was a little difficult the way I reacted, but something bizarre like that would shocked anybody who got the front row seat witnessing it. As everything settles in me, I realize that their intention to help wasn't bad but it is more of my personal faith that makes it difficult for me to comprehend and accept the legitimacy of their actions. I guess it's better for Eric and me not to see each other for a while.

Mark becomes my regular lunch mate. And we go out once in a while whenever my schedule permits it. He's the sweetest man I've ever met and he has all the qualities of a true gentleman.

Weeks pass, and burying myself at work helps get my mind off Eric. I sometimes put in more hours than what my body can handle just to occupy myself.

One morning in December, as I'm driving to work, my vision starts to swirl then I lose control of the steering wheel. The car starts to swerve. The automatic break control system in my car is useless on the frigid slippery icy road. I'm able to glance quickly at my rearview mirror and witness in shock, the cars behind me are scrambling to avoid colliding to each other. Luckily the left fast lane is clear when my car spins one time before it plows on the concrete traffic barriers. Before my car stops skidding, my world blacks out.

My car seat is equipped with a heartbeat detector system that made it easier for the emergency rescuers to know the severity of my condition.

When I open my eyes, I'm in a familiar place months ago but it was Mary lying in the bed then. And another familiar thing is the person standing beside my bed. "Hi, there my dear!" my father greets with a million dollar smile in his face that I have not seen before. "Do you remember how you got the scar on your forehead?"

I don't know why my father asked me that out of the blue but I answer anyway, "Yeah, my childhood friend, Lucy, accidentally poked me with the metal tip of the umbrella while we were playing with it."

My father hugs me as tight as he can like everything will be fine now, then my mother joins in with tears in her eyes. It feels like everything is déjà vu.

Then, another familiar face appears, it's Eric. My father pulls away and says, "We'll leave you two for a while."

"Hi!" he says smiling in the most attractive way any woman could get hypnotized.

"Dr. Love's coat came in handy," he says grinning about what had transpired. "Good thing I didn't burn it. Anyway, Thea and Zian wanted to stay longer but they need to head back to New Mexico. Their wait is over. It's time for them to go home."

"How long have I've been here?" I ask.

"It's your fifth day today," he answers.

— 0 —

Three Days Ago

It was midnight when Thea noticed a blinking green light coming from the closet. The light was visible through the tiny gap between the closet doors. She jumped off the bed for she knew that there was only one thing making that light…the rod!

She held the rod with her right hand pointing the crystal end up. Immediately it started to project an image of a man. "Thea, Gaulleo is finally defeated! It's time for you and our son to come home. I'm giving you 45 days to complete your journey back here. If you don't arrive at the given time then we will come to get the two of you," the man said.

The next day, Thea phoned Eric about the good news, "It finally happened. We're going home! Zian and I will be heading to the Gallery."

"That's wonderful! I'll go with you. Just give me a day to get to Tally," Eric requested.

He called Tally on her cell phone and home phone but she didn't answer. He left messages that he needed to talk to her. It wasn't in his character to just give up until all possibilities were tried. He went to her apartment and work and both hit a wall. He then decided to give her one day to respond.

Noon the next day, he couldn't wait any longer for Tally to call, so he took the courage to show up to her parents' diner.

When he got to the diner, a sign hanging at the door that said, 'We're Closed' disheartened him. Still he knocked on the door to check if anybody was in. He would take anyone to point him in Tally's direction.

He breathed a sigh of relief when the door opened and a man in his 70's appeared.

"I'm sorry but we're closed for the day," the man said while trying to put on his warm jacket indicative of someone who was about to head out.

"Oh, hi! My name is Eric Dutton and I'm Tally's friend. I've been trying to get a hold of her since yesterday but I didn't have any luck. I just want to make sure that everything is fine with her. Sir, if you don't mind, maybe you can tell me where I can get a hold of her?" he asked.

But the man didn't answer right away. "Please, Sir. I really need to talk to her," he pleaded.

"My daughter had an accident three days ago. She's at the Angel of Mercy Hospital right now. We're just about to head there," Mr. McDowell said in a very down voice.

"An accident!" Eric exclaimed. "Is she alright?

What happened?" he barraged the man with questions.

"She passed out while driving to work. Maybe she had been working straight hours more than she thought she could handle trying to finish a project...I'm sorry but I can't tell you anything more," Mr. McDowell said with skepticism about who the man he was speaking to.

"I'd like to visit her tonight, if it's alright with you?" Eric asked.

"Not a problem. But I don't think that's a good idea since she will be undergoing an operation in two hours. She might not be ready to wake up and entertain anybody tonight. As a matter of fact, we will only be staying during the operation to be there when it finishes so the doctor can update us of her condition," the father said, giving Eric a hint of discouragement.

"Nice meeting you, Sir," he shook Mr. McDowell's hand and left.

That night he met with Thea. He told her what had happened to Tally and they knew what they needed to do that night.

Luckily, the drugs in Tally's system took a while to wear off and Eric got the chance to pick up her parents before she came out of it. He made it looked like that during his visit in the early morning their daughter started to wake up. He told them to make sure to ask her a question only they and she knew the answer to, to check if her memory was affected.

— ∅ —

"So, did I get the healing light?" I ask in my weakest voice struggling with a smile.

Eric smiles back and says, "So for someone who has an idea about what went on, how did it feel?"

"I saw what was happening around midnight last night when Thea, Zian and you came to visit. I thought I was only dreaming but then I realized when I saw Thea started to place her hand on my head that I needed to go back into my body or at least try harder to awaken myself. That was when I opened my I eyes and saw my father," I say struggling hard to remember everything. "But I can't remember anything that happened after Thea placed her hand on me."

"Also, the odd part was I remember being at a different room. It was dusky, a lot colder and faced with stainless steel doors. Maybe that was the only dream part of it all."

Eric's face suddenly turns serious then he speaks, "I wanted to let you know that I will be going away for a while to help Thea and Zian in any way I can, though...I know they're pretty much equipped themselves to tackle anything, and I might just end up lagging them behind. But I still would like to be there to say my goodbyes and to make sure they'll be taking off on the Morsel safely."

"Sometimes it doesn't take power to help. Standing up for them to show that you care brings out the superhero that you are," I say trying to let him know that I'm supporting his humble spirit.

He then touches my hand and sincerely says, "Thank you for everything."

I smile at him. Then he starts to slowly pull his hand away. He turns around then heads to the door.

This is one situation where I need superpower myself to get off this bed and give him a hug if this is the last time we ever going to see each other. Instead, I take all the strength inside of me and utter in my loudest voice for him to hear, "Try not to die!"

I know what they will be faced with. Flying that thing out of there is like taking the fire out of the dragon.

He looks back at me and gives me one nod of confirmation. After he disappears behind the door, I feel that something in me left with him. I guess when you start to fall for someone you tend not to judge. I can strongly feel that he's holding back something.

The next day, every part of me feels great. Even the doctors are surprised. The surprise reaction from doctors I can take but what really bothers me is the creepy look that every staff member at the hospital gives me. Sometimes when a nurse comes in to check on me, a group of them will obviously stop and steal a glance in my room like there's some kind of freak show going on. That's when I decide to request to be discharged the same day and walk out of the hospital feeling relieved.

Monday, January 20, 2031. My vacation with friends, and New Year came and went, but I can't seem to get my mind off Eric. When I'm with friends, I'll be merry and often rock my three inch boogie shoes all night long but then when I get home and all alone my mind will end up thinking about him. And when I'm with Mark, I feel so special and cared for but then again I wonder how it would feel with Eric. It's a cycle that's hard to get by.

One day, I take the courage to give him a call on his cellphone. On my first try, he doesn't answer. Then I try a second time, and again no answer. I say to myself that after the third try and he doesn't answer then I'll take that as a sign and will never try again. My third attempt fails and I retreat. But at the back of my mind I'm thinking, what if he doesn't have his old phone anymore or worse, he's in trouble and can't pick up. Now that makes me restless.

After an hour, my phone rings. It's Eric! I almost drop my phone from excitement but then I calm myself down and answer, "Hello!"

"Tally? It's me Eric. Did you call?" he asks.

"Oh, yes! I just want to know how are Thea and Zian doing? Or have they left already?" I ask controlling myself not to ask how he's doing.

"They're both excited and couldn't be happier since their homecoming is within their grasp at last," he answers. "Luckily, I was able to get the three slots for a tour at The Gallery on the 3rd of February. It's really limited and expensive. Now there's a year wait to get in. By the way how are you doing?"

"Well, it's a little slow here with inches of snow and negative temp. But I'm happy to be back kicking. What about you?" I ask.

"I like it here. I can't complain about the change of weather and surroundings. You should see the mountains' brilliant colors of pink and green at sunset just outside the city. You know you can come here and visit us anytime you want," he invites pausing for a second for my answer. "But I know you are married to your work so just stay warm and drive safely."

"Say hi to Thea and Zian for me," I say.

"Will do. I'll talk to you later then," he replies.

I'm meaning to make him promise to keep in touch, but in return I say, "Okay, bye!" Then I hang up.

CHAPTER 21

Gaulleo's Realm

Gaulkan exists a galaxy apart from Earth in the universe. Aside from the powerful screams of its little children that could leave anyone hearing impaired, no other power exists in its people and leader. Their high intelligence, perpetual wisdoms and pure intentions are just a few of their characteristics that made them worthy of living in this holy ground.

Powers will only be sent from a Higher Being only when the order in its world is disturbed. And only one deserving Gaulkanian will be chosen to lead and bring the order back.

Gaulkanians live like humans live on Earth, but with perfect harmony. No weapons of mass destruction or even any sorts of small weapons need to exist. No uprise, until...

December 17, 2030 – A Month Earlier

The evil befell their leader Gaulleo, decades ago when the sky turned dark, the wind stopped blowing and the sea dried up but only for a day, and yet the darkness in Gaulleo's heart exists to this day.

It was raining in the middle of the night when the Watcher of the Primal Versi came rushing to Lukan's house. Upon hearing the man pounding on his front door, he jumped out of his bed and ran down the stairs to open the door. The Watcher, dripping wet and out of breath, retracted his tongue back into his mouth then gulped and said, "They're coming to Millopin's!"

"Hurry and tell the others and I will meet you at the Patrum," Lukan commanded.

The Patrum was an open field that they used at night for large gatherings of the group Primal Versi.

But the watcher who hadn't recovered his regular breathing yet from running asked Lukan, "Can I walk?"

His leader just looked at him without blinking

and said, "You want me to call on the lightning for you to run?"

"I'll meet you at the Patruuuuum!" the Watcher replied while running away and fading in the rain.

Lukan ran back upstairs to wake up his teenage son, Mati. He first wiped the drool off the side of his son's face then shook him gently on his shoulder then said, "We need to go. There will be a gathering at the Patrum."

The son still drowsy in sleepiness negotiated, "Pleeease five more minutes."

"You want me to call on the thunder for you to wake up?" the son immediately sat up, hit his head on the top bunk bed then got dressed.

Lukan was the leader of Primal Versi, whose mission was to take Gaulleo out of power. When he and his son arrived at the meeting place, a man came forward and said to them, "We're too late. The entire Millopins were taken."

Lukan couldn't believe what he just heard. He then turned his attention to the crowd gathered behind the man and saw the look of sadness and desperation in their faces. Then turned back to the man in front of him and asked, "What happened?

Why did they take the whole family this time?"

With disbelief, the man replied, "Someone told Gaulleo that the Millopin had been breaking the law. The family hid the fact that they had their second child 30 years ago. Now, there's a big possibility that everyone who participated in the same act would be dealt with the same force."

With the grim reality that it won't be long before the group could be discovered, Lukan quickly thought of a plan. He walked toward the crowd and said, "I have an idea that might work, but I want everyone to agree otherwise we will not proceed. We attempted and failed in the past to stop them at our doors but this time we will all march together into Gaulleo's empire and face them on his ground.

"Let's meet tomorrow at midnight at The Cellar. I will tell you my plan then we will cast our votes."

The next day, everyone started to arrive at The Cellar around midnight. The place was like an underground hub where narrow tunnels, exact fit of a person to walk through, branched in and out of it. The tunnels were painstakingly built by members to give them access right from their homes and some secluded places to The Cellar to avoid detection. And this hub was right beneath Lukan's house. And that was where he secretly built the Morsel with Usil's help.

Right after Thea left, Lukan committed the place to the group.

After the meeting was concluded, Lukan requested for the women to stay behind and the rest started to prepare for their planned attack.

Right before dawn the next day, hundreds gathered at the Patrum. The group was divided into two sections, the first was the line of offense, and the second was the reinforcement. The entire first line of offense wore full helmets which covered the faces and were never before practiced in Gaulkan since covering of one's face was considered an act of cowardice. To them, you shouldn't hide behind a mask if you truly believed with your heart in what you were fighting for.

They marched for miles without any weapons, not even tools to protect themselves. They stopped before reaching the border between the land of the ordinary Gaulkanians and Gaulleo's forbidden land.

Surprising enough Gaulleo's battalion of army was waiting for their arrival and blocking them to move in any further. When Gaulleo saw that the

Primal Versi continued to march on and was getting closer to his land and not stopping, scared of his army, he gave his first order, "On guard!"

His front line of soldiers placed their hands on the handle of their swords to warn the incoming group. The marching group stopped less than 50 feet short to the border and now standing face to face with Gaulleo's army. Lukan immediately gave his first command, "Re-order!"

The front line started to shuffle their positions. Some stayed in their places and the others stepped back and moved from side to side as if looking for their match across the field. When Gaulleo finally got a closer look of what was in front of them, he furiously asked the leader of his army standing beside him, "Are those what I think they are?!"

"You are not mistaken, my Lord. They are indeed wearing full helmets," the soldier replied.

Confused with what he was witnessing, he asked, "And what are they doing now?"

"I've never seen such tactics before. Maybe, that's what they call *flash mob* in the other world," the soldier answered, puzzled like his master.

When the shuffle stopped, Lukan

commanded, "On guard!"

The group placed their hands on the sides of the helmets as if about to trigger something. Gaulleo felt that something not good was about to happen.

Standing on the balcony of his castle looking into the field, he ordered his men, "Attack!"

His army drew their swords out. At the same time the Primal Versi's front line started to lift their helmets then took them off and dropped them on the ground.

The army ready to charge didn't take a step forward. They stood still, faces turning white like they had seen something unexpected and beaming bright right in front of them.

"What are you waiting for? Destroy them!" shouted Gaulleo.

One soldier started charging straight ahead holding his sword, and then stopped right in front of the one standing across him. He dropped his sword then wrapped his arms tightly around the person and said, "Mother!"

Gaulleo's army was consisting of grownup sons and daughters taken away from the mothers standing right across the battlefield.

Then the rest of the soldiers in the front line started running except for one who didn't seem to spot anyone familiar to him.

Gaulleo was turning red in the face. He collared his right-hand man and angrily said, "Go out there and stop those simpletons right now!!!" The man scampered away.

The rest of his army dropped their weapons and walked away from his dominion.

On the field, one woman in her 70's from Lukan's reinforcement group started to walk towards the other side and straight to the one left standing with his sword. She extended her hand to ask the young man to surrender his sword to her. The young man didn't move. He stared at the woman, raised his sword then struck it down to the ground.

The woman gave the boy a warm hug and whispered in his ear, "I'm your grandmother."

After the last child surrendered, Gaulleo screamed looking up in the sky with his both hands up in the air like challenging someone above, "Nooooooo!"

At that instant, a lightning bolt struck him and threw him off against the wall behind him. He dropped on the floor unconscious. Lukan, who was able to sneak inside the castle, walked up to him, knelt down, and then held him in his arms and uttered, "Gaulleo, wake up."

Gaulleo started to open his eyes. His face brightened up. He lost the darkness around his eyes and then asked, "Where am I?"

"Here in Gaulkan with your people," Lukan answered.

"I was lost in a dark place where a stream of fire was running like river and I was walking on the side trying to find my way home. Then I saw my mother, who had been dead for centuries, and she told me to walk with her and that was when I heard you speak to wake me up," he recalled.

~ σ ~

Lukan is now the new leader of Gaulkan. Gaulleo's faith was compromised when the dark entity from Ganti took over him, thus by law will not be permitted to lead but to follow.

CHAPTER 22

The Gallery

Present Day 2031 — Albuquerque, New Mexico

Eric knows who to meet with to make sure they'll cover everything on the day of the tour. David, being the second guy in-charge of the Morsel at The Gallery, will give him accurate descriptions of its structure and security. But he wants to make sure not to involve his friend for his own good. So, he schedules a meeting with David a week before their tour.

The three are staying at Jane's old house that is currently not occupied since Jane died the summer of 1990. Thea and Zian were included in the woman's will to have the right to her house since she considered them as family and they lived with her for a long time. Jane took Thea in from the shelter house when she was pregnant with Zian. The boy grew up considering her as his grandma. And they stayed with her until the time that they needed to move to Minnesota. It was during their tour of the Oakland city by the river on a ferry with Eric when they knew something had happened to her. The woman died of a heart attack at age of 98 that day. They went to her funeral and it was during the reading of her will that they found out that Jane left them the house. But they couldn't live there at that time because of their urgent mission to look for the Morsel in Minnesota.

David is currently in New Mexico checking on the Capsule that is on display at the museum. He makes sure that the people touring The Gallery are not causing any damage to it.

Eric didn't tell his friend anything about Thea and Zian. For him, the fewer people who know, the easier to protect them.

The two hug when they see each other. After they settle down, Eric starts by saying, "I called you because my friends and I were able to get passes next month for a tour at The Gallery. I was thinking since I'm in town why not get in touch with you and check how you and your family are doing?"

"I'm really glad to see you. Anne and Emily are both doing fine. And my work here will be completed after your scheduled tour then will come back again next month," David says.

"Speaking of your work, I'm just curious, are your organization or the government not wary of that thing getting stolen? That thing is so grand to just sit there open for viewing by anyone whose intention you don't even know," Eric curiously asks.

"Good luck to anyone who can fly that thing out of there! The Capsule is missing one important piece to fly. It's some kind of fuse or key in cylindrical shape that we can't duplicate at all. Turning its system on is the easy part that the Mechanic was able to do. But the taking off is the difficulty we encountered and up to now can't figure out. The prototypes are the ones we can maneuver but that original piece at The Gallery is still a work in progress. Also, before any attacks could happen they will be detected miles before they even get closed to The Gallery. And that will be as close as they can get because there are ready missiles to bring them down," David doesn't show any hesitation spilling all details about the vehicle and the place.

"It sounds a lot of fun. No wonder you don't want to leave your job at the company. How did they manage to bring the Capsule into The Gallery?" He discreetly segues to the direction of how Thea can fly the Morsel out of the place without causing too much damage or injuries.

It's possible on the day of their tour that children may be in attendance, so Eric wants to make sure that their plan will proceed with extra caution.

"The Gallery has a dome in the center that opens like four metal petals. The Capsule was lifted in the air and brought down through the dome. But the switch to the dome is in a box secured by a four digit code which I designed. Everything is well thought out. Anyway, enough about me, so what's been keeping you busy aside from your curiosity about the Capsule?" David asks.

"I'm doing architectural consulting on contractual basis nowadays. Currently, I'm between assignments. The nice thing about consulting is after every job I get to enjoy some time off with friends like now to get a glimpse of the much talked about Capsule," he replies.

"You know I can take you in anytime you want since I have the authority to go in and out whenever I want. But it has to be just you. I can't have your friends in for now," David offers.

"Wow! That would be great!" Eric excitedly blurts out.

On their way to the museum, he asks David in passing, "So how are the Farmer and the Prophet doing?"

"A new guy is now in charge of the Greenhouse. The Prophet's program will be delayed for a year or two to satisfy the committee's additional requirements. He needs to suppress certain element in his vaccine to make sure it will not cause wayward side effects to his subjects," David narrates.

Eric is rejoicing inside him after hearing that piece of information. All his effort warning the committee about the Prophet's work didn't go in vain.

The entrance gate to the museum is guarded by heavily armed military men. The gate has a big fort that seems to conceal an important weapon to keep the place secure. They validate and phone in David's id before they let them pass. The entire area is gated with tall metal fence with spear-like tips. After which they drive for a mile before reaching the museum.

The Gallery is a huge squared structure with a dome in the center. The public parking is just at the front side of the building. The sides and back area are reserved for authorized vehicles and personnel only. Given that David has a high security level, they drive all the way to the back and park at a green lot with a sign that has David's name on it. Cameras are everywhere and all doors have security locks.

After David swipes his ID card at the security box located beside the back door, a yellow light appears. He then takes a step back and a blue light coming from the box scans him from head to toe then a green light appears on it. He quickly grabs the door's metal handle, turns it upward and it opens.

If the Gallery looks boxy in the outside, the inside contrasts with its arched architecture. David shows him first the hallway from the visitor's entrance. It has glass cabinets along the walls that display the history of the Capsule and some old black and white pictures taken when it crashed. The people who worked on it were shown on the pictures too. And only someone who knows David well can recognize him in one of the pictures.

On their way to the main attraction, David whispers to him, "All exterior sides of this buildings and the roof have hidden machine guns that are remotely controlled."

Eric is thinking to himself, *how in the world then can I avoid being shot that day?* But instead he utters, "That is so reassuring."

Finally, at the center of the museum, resting directly on the marble floor and right under the fifty foot high dome is the magnificent piece of shiny silvery bluish tint metallic object! The shape of it reminds him of a car rooftop cargo carrier box but a lot complicated and grand in its entirety.

It is surrounded by red velvet ropes and gold stanchions 20 feet away to prevent the crowd from getting close to it. "During the tour, there will be two security men guarding the Capsule. Anyone who behaves in a disorderly way will be taken out of the museum," David warns.

As Eric discreetly checks the area from wall to wall, he notices on one of the walls a glass switch box with a number pad on it. Inside is a round red button two inches in diameter. He realizes that it could be the switch button to open the dome. The position of it is about his friend's height of six feet. All he needs to figure out is the code to unlock the box. Else he seriously needs a contingency plan if he fails.

The vehicle's aerodynamic design helps tell which part is the front. And the dark tinted glassy area located on top of the frontend could be the pilot's window, Eric assumes.

There's a stainless steel stand with a glass container on top placed behind one of the velvet ropes. The glass contains the descriptions that tell the characteristics of the Morsel; and the most awaited one, the black and white picture of the occupant lying in a glass coffin. It was identified that the Capsule's body contains two main elements which are iridium and osmium and the rest is still unknown to human science. It has dimensions of 15 feet long, 10 feet wide, 8 feet in height, weighs 3 tons; and speed is immeasurable. It can be piloted by two crew members and one pod is still intact. The roughness of its surface makes it looking more like a chunk of meteorite. But no details are mentioned about the occupant's characteristics and where it's currently being kept except that it didn't survive the crash. Both David and Eric know that it's being preserved still in the cold chamber, and whether it's still alive or not, only the Prophet knows.

Eric now has a clear idea what Usil looked like. And it's no different than a human male.

They concluded their tour by going to the lower level where David points to a door that leads to the control room where all the security monitoring systems are located.

CHAPTER 23

Homeward Bound

February 3, 2031; the tour at The Gallery starts exactly at nine in the morning. It is going smoothly at the entrance hallway displays, when the room suddenly turns dark. The children scream and the adults panic to grab on all the children together. It turns out that a second grade class is having an honorary tour that same day. Thea, Zian and Eric are standing behind the crowd.

Eric holds his cane horizontally with both hands as if about to break it in half. He starts to twist and turn one half to the right until it comes loose and the cane splits. "Zian, take this and don't lose it no matter what. Your mother will ask for it when it's time," he instructs the boy.

The two security men, who have flashlights with them, split up; one goes to the crowd to keep the order, and the other runs outside to call for help.

But when the security man steps out of the building, he's surprised to see that all lights on the posts are on. Confused whether there's power outage in the area or just malfunctions in the light switches inside, he then goes back in.

Thea and Zian quietly hurry in the direction of the Morsel. Eric goes to the lower level to jam the door of the security control room with a little spark coming from his finger. He then runs back up to the switch box to open the dome for the Morsel to get out without any trouble. He punches 0604 for June 4, Emily's birth month and day. It didn't work. He then enters 0690, for the month and year of birth. Still, it doesn't do it. He is still working on unlocking the box when an unusual sound starts to reverberate in the room.

The Morsel starts to shine like a gem and it brightens the room.

When the children see the lights coming from the center of the museum just ahead of them they start to scurry to it. The children's screams are replaced with wows and excitement. Everybody thought that what's happening is still part of the museum's attraction. They are all ecstatic when they realize that it is the Capsule that's doing the tricks.

What they don't realize is that Thea and Zian

were able to sneak inside and are getting ready to fly it. "Zian, hand me the cane," Thea asks, seated in the pilot's chair her right hand waiting for the boy, seated to her right, to pass the cane.

The boy hands the half of what was given to him by Eric. Thea then turns the one end of the half cane until the portion that she is turning comes off. Inside the half of the cane is the rod! She slides the rod out of the cane then presses it gently in a vertical position into a semi-cylindrical holder in the center of the front panel where numerous displays and gauges about the Morsel's performance are shown. It fits perfectly!

The huge size of the vehicle covers what's taking place behind it...Eric having a hard time unlocking the switch box. But one guard left at the site going around the Morsel to see what's going on to it, sees him. The guard starts running towards him and then jumps him.

The guard is on top of him pinning him down to the floor on his back when he sees a woman appearing out of nowhere and calls out to him, "Eric, what should I do?"

"Tally?! What are you doing here?" he struggles to ask while scuffling with the guard.

"You didn't think I'm just gonna let them go without saying goodbye? Wouldn't miss this for the world! Now tell me what I need to do!" I shout back.

My attention is split between the scene of the fight and the amazing object I've never seen before. Then I feel a mild vibration on the floor. It's the Morsel. It's starting to lift off the ground.

"My cane! Over there!" he points to the ground on my right below the switch box.

I run to it, pick it up and ask Eric, "What happened to the rest of the cane or have your legs shrunk?"

"You can ask later. For now, twist the handle!" he instructs me between exchanges of punches.

I twist the handle while holding firmly on the stick side of the cane. The handle starts to loosen and then comes off. The remaining piece of the cane reveals a high-carbon steel tip that is pointed enough to shatter any glass.

"Use it to break the switch box on the wall just above you then press the red button!" he shouts while this time he's on top pinning the security guy down.

I hold on to it with both hands like the way I hold on to an icepick ready to break ice but this time I aim straight at the switch box avoiding the number pad. Then I tighten my grip, pull my hands up over my head and give all that I have striking hard the glass and breaking it into piece. I immediately press the red button and the dome starts to open.

The Morsel starts to rise up. The crowd goes wild at the spectacular show that's happening right in front of them and doesn't even notice the commotion across the room.

Suddenly, I'm pushed from behind and fall on the floor. I look back and see the second guard pressing the red button.

The dome starts to close back and the crowd cries, "Oh, no!" But the Morsel, half way out already, then blasts its way out right before the dome fully closes.

By this time, Eric successfully knocks out the one guard. He runs to me, helps me stand up and says, "Come on! We need to go!"

The lights miraculously turn back on in the building. Everybody is getting frantic to go outside to see where the Morsel goes.

Eric holds on to my hand tightly like holding

a child afraid to lose her in the crowd. Then my phone rings. I reach for it, and blurt out, "It's Mark calling!"

"Huh? Who's Mark?" Eric questions.

I answer the phone and start saying, "Oh, snap! I forgot about the lunch. I'm sorry, something came up..."

"I don't think this is a good time to chat!" Eric sighs while we scurry to the exit.

"Where are you? Who was that guy?" Mark asks with concern if not jealous. "Are you ok?"

"Mark, I'll explain later, I need to run," I say then hang up.

When we get outside, we see a lot of flashing vehicles starting to pull up in the parking area then stop right before where the crowd gathers looking up and watching as the special object hovers 150 feet above The Gallery.

Military men get out of the vehicles and start to push and instruct everybody to go back inside the museum. The adults, in charge of the children, start to grab and lead all the kids back inside. But the kids are getting out of control trying to push back like a school of fish to see the magnificent object floating in the sky.

Eric grabs onto my arm and gently pulls me away from the crowd and we sneak behind the closest flashing vehicle.

The Morsel stays in place for a few minutes then starts to fly away up into the sky.

The children are cheering and shouting, "Wait! Come back!"

As we watch intently as it gets smaller and smaller like a dot in the cloud, Eric reaches for my hand and gently holds on to it. And when I look at him, tears are running down his face. He's happy that Thea and Zian are heading home but at the same time feeling the pain of missing them already. I grip his hand tightly as if letting him know that he's not alone.

By the time the object disappears, the securities and extra military men on the ground still don't know what to do. I hear that they're instructed to hold their weapons down.

"Let's get out of here," Eric whispers.

The next day, Gen. Bauman is taken out of the box and back to the population. He is granted one call outside.

"Hello! This is General Bauman," he says.

"Yes, Sir! Good morning!" the Mechanic answers.

"How did it go?" the General asks.

"As you warned in your letter, someone attempted to steal and fly the Capsule just yesterday," the Mechanic answers.

"Did you make the switch? Did you stop it?" the General follows up.

"Well, something went wrong. I instructed my men to replace it with the prototype that I could control remotely, but it turned out that the switch didn't happen. What I don't understand, Sir, is why you wanted the person to get inside the Capsule instead of stopping him or her before, and not sacrifice one expensive prototype?" the Mechanic questioning the General's intention.

"I wanted to make sure that the one who would attempt to fly it was the person I'd been looking for. She had in her possession the missing piece to fly the Morsel, I meant the Capsule. And you just failed me and the organization you swore to serve," the General then hangs up.

Eric is now back in the cycle that he once

attributed as his curse. But for the first time, he feels good about it. He sees it as an opportunity to help and be a morsel of hope for anyone who needs one.

And on my part, I'm starting to enjoy all the life's possibilities; and that includes getting to know Eric better. Having a wider perspective helps me see the magic in his inorganic world and appreciate the beauty of his unique being.